Running from Shame

Crawdad Beach Series (Book 9)

Lisa Buffaloe

Running from Shame

Visit the author's website at https://lisabuffaloe.com.

Cover Design: JoAnn Durgin

ISBN: 978-1-957715-40-7 (eBook)
ISBN: 978-1-957715-41-4 (Paperback)
ISBN: 978-1-957715-42-1 (Hardcover)

Running from Shame

Shame drove her away,
God's grace brought her home.

Ashamed and heartbroken, Brooke Taylor ran from the only place she'd called home. As a skilled craftsman, she could fix practically any item, but no matter what she did, she couldn't fix her past. For ten years, Brooke stayed busy and hid from the world, but when her workplace shut down, Brooke had to make a choice. Would she run again or return to Crawdad Beach?

A wicked hit on the football field changed Tate Tillman's plans for college and his hope of playing in the NFL. His career choices redirected, Tate crisscrossed the country as a contract welder. When his cousin made him an offer to join him in Crawdad Beach, Tate didn't refuse. Yet, no matter where he went, that night continued to haunt him.

As friendship forms between Brooke and Tate, will they be given a new start, or will shame and guilt keep them from God's grace and their future?

Book 9 of the Crawdad Beach Series

Each book in the series may be enjoyed as a standalone.

Table of Contents

Chapter 1

Refusing to cry, Brooke Taylor kept her head down as she swept the floor of the now-empty building. Crying never did any good, anyway. She learned that painful fact in multiple foster homes.

"You don't need to clean anymore. The building is sold and will be torn down to make way for another restaurant. You're welcome to join us in Florida." Fenton McAdam's gentle voice usually soothed her, but not today.

Just to keep herself busy, Brooke continued sweeping. Fenton and his wife had taken her in when she was at her lowest, given her a safe workplace, and even provided the apartment on the second floor above the workshop where she stayed.

Brooke couldn't fault the man for closing his shop so he could retire. She knew it would happen. He'd saved for years to purchase a place on the coast so he and his wife could spend his retirement fishing.

"If you stay here, you know the guys will watch out for you," Fenton said.

Brooke squeezed her eyes shut, trying to stop the tears. Fenton's friends were Christians, good guys who treated her like big brothers. The men had met every Wednesday night in the shop for Bible study and then gathered with their families at Fenton's house on the weekend to watch sports. They had always made her feel welcome.

Brooke pasted on a smile as she turned toward Fenton and studied his face. She wanted always to remember the man who had been so very kind to her. "You won't be opening another shop. There's nothing for me here or in Florida. Unless I need to be there to make sure you don't wear speedos and black socks with sandals."

He chuckled. "You don't have to worry about that. Maybe it's time for you to go home," Fenton's kind voice prodded. "From what little you've shared about your adopted parents, I believe they would welcome your return with open arms."

Brooke turned her back so he wouldn't see her stupid trembling lip. "You don't understand. I've messed up too bad ever to go back again."

"It's never too late to return home. Promise me you will pray about where you'll go, and please keep us updated."

She nodded. "I promise." She scrubbed the broom bristles over an old oil stain. Her life was too stained to return to the Taylors. They'd adopted her out of foster care, given her a good home, and even their name. They'd always been kind and loving, but she never deserved their love.

Besides the mess she'd made in high school, once she flunked out of her first semester in college, she'd packed her car and headed for Nashville. With so many people wanting to be country-western stars, Brooke figured she could find work in the busy town.

She'd gone from working in bars and restaurants, even doing temp work in offices, until finally finding a home with Fenton's small engine and bike repair shop. She'd always been good with her hands and enjoyed tinkering with machines and fixing things.

But what would she do now, and where could she go?

Tate Tillman rubbed a hand over his close-cropped beard as he stood on the sidewalk of Crawdad Beach's Main Street. What kind of crazy place had he found himself in? Who named their business with funny names like Doohickeys Hardware, Knick Knacks Antique, Tiddlywinks Restaurant, Rolling in the Dough Bakery, Curl and Dye Beauty Shop, and Hotel de Crawdad? At least the loft apartments, law office, medical clinic, and post office looked normal.

The little town was busy with people and cars as though it was a destination place. Why? The two-story buildings were well-maintained, and the brick-paved street was pretty cool, but why were so many people in a town that wasn't even located on the beach?

He stopped to stare at a young couple walking a massive cat on a leash. What added to the strangeness was that a silver-haired gentleman walking next to them had a little white and black dog. The animals seemed even to enjoy being together.

His cousin, Jeremy, who owned Knick Knacks Antiques,

said it was a great place to live and had offered Tate the opportunity to set up a shop on property Jeremy had inherited.

Tate couldn't believe his luck. After graduating from trade school, he'd traveled the country taking on welding jobs. His own building would finally allow him to venture into the artistic side of welding and metal fabrication.

The sound of a lawnmower jerked Tate's attention to the street. A lady wearing a bright pink jogging suit was hunched down as though racing her mower as she putted down the road. People waved and called her name as though this was normal behavior.

Tate chuckled. With all the weird stuff in his background, maybe he would fit right in, and maybe, just maybe, he'd finally found a place to call home.

Chapter 2

Brooke continued driving southeast on the interstate. The little trailer hitched behind her car sure wasn't helping her gas mileage. She'd been traveling for hours and still hadn't decided where to go. Since it was late January, she did not want to move further north than where she'd lived in Nashville.

Maybe she should have gone to Florida with Fenton and his wife. At least it would be warmer. Brooke would miss the couple, but they needed time together. They didn't need a tag-along misfit like her. No one did. Her birth mom had been a drug-addicted prostitute who died in jail, and her birth dad gave up his parental rights. As a result, Brooke's first fourteen years were spent in foster care.

Fenton had often told Brooke she needed to pray, but what good would that do if she did? She'd prayed plenty of times when she was a kid, and that never seemed to help.

Brooke groaned. That wasn't entirely true. She believed prayer worked when she lived in Crawdad Beach with Chester and Maybelline Taylor. They'd already raised their family when they adopted Brooke, but she never believed she deserved a nice couple like them as parents.

Yet for the last ten years, the couple had continued to

leave Brooke messages on her phone and texted her, saying they loved her and were praying for her. She never acknowledged them; she just couldn't. They didn't know everything she'd done, all the rotten things others had done to her, and the rotten things she'd done.

Brooke stared at the road ahead. She'd saved some money, but the thought of moving somewhere without knowing anyone and not having a job made her skin crawl. The years on her own in Nashville had been a nightmare until Fenton hired her, kept her safe, and allowed her the opportunity to have a job and hide from the world.

Two sports cars raced past her car. Brooke increased her speed. The trailer shimmied behind her vehicle, causing her to slow down and stay in the right-hand lane. Why was she in a hurry? She didn't even know where she was heading.

Fenton had asked her to pray about where she was going. If she prayed for guidance, would God help her? Probably not, but maybe it was worth a try.

Brooke shot up a quick prayer and flipped on the car radio. A song about going home came through the speakers. Brooke rolled her eyes. Surely, that was just a coincidence. She turned off the radio and stared ahead at the fast-moving traffic.

A moving van moved in her lane in front of her car. The words emblazoned on the back of the truck read *There's no place like home*.

Seriously? Brooke growled and changed lanes so she didn't have to see the sign.

Going back to Crawdad Beach wasn't an option, was it? Chester and Maybelline said they loved her no matter what, but could that be true? What would they do if she showed up on their doorstep?

Brooke continued driving. Since she didn't have anywhere else to go, she might as well give it a try. She could always hit the road again if it didn't work out.

Spotting an exit, Brooke pulled into a gas station to fill up and plot her course to the only place she'd ever called home.

A small bell over the door dinged as Tate stepped into Knick Knacks Antiques. He glanced around the old building crowded with furniture, glassware, antique jewelry, art, and old toys. His metal artwork might fit right in.

"You made it!" Jeremy hurried toward Tate and gave him a high-five.

Jeremy's wife, Grace, gave Tate a shy but friendly smile. He could understand how the beauty, with long brunette hair and big brown eyes, had captured his cousin's attention.

"Welcome to Crawdad Beach," Grace said. "Jeremy has told me so much about you."

"I'm not sure if I should be pleased or worried." Tate chuckled. "We had fun growing up down the street from one another."

"Fun?" Jeremy laughed as he bopped Jeremy's shoulder. "We were always in trouble from the crazy stunts we tried.

We had a blast together. But, then this guy," Jeremy pointed to Tate, "started football and became a superstar."

Tate shook his head. "Until my leg got mangled on the last game of the season." Besides the pain of the injury, he'd lost his full-ride college scholarship and hopes of ever playing in the NFL.

"Yeah, that was a wicked hit you took." Jeremy grimaced. "I still think the guy who tackled you should have faced charges for the way he tried to twist your leg off. How's it doing?"

"Still hurts at times." Tate knew his cousin understood since he'd messed up his leg while landing on a parachute jump in the military. "How about you?"

"Same. Just one of those things, I guess. You ready to see the shop?" Jeremy turned to his wife. "You okay with me leaving you for a little while?"

"I'll be fine." Grace rubbed her rounded belly as she turned her gaze toward Tate. "He's worried the baby will come at any moment."

Jeremy took her in his arms. "You only have another week." They looked at one another, all dreamy-eyed and mushy-like. They even kissed.

Tate turned away. He was happy about his cousin's good fortune with a loving wife and baby on the way, but their mutual affection for one another only made him regret his past choices all the more. He doubted anyone would love him like that. "Get a room," Tate half-joked.

"Oh, we did." Jeremy smiled wide enough that practically

all his teeth showed. "Worked out very nicely, thank you very much. You should try it."

Tate shrugged. "Haven't found the right girl yet." He'd met a few possibilities, but he didn't think he was worthy, not after what happened with that one young woman.

"Because you've been too busy traveling from place to place."

"Hey, I wanted to see the country. I didn't want to stay in Chicagoland like our parents, grandparents, and other relatives." Tate's parents were good, hardworking, blue-collar people who lived in the same house that had belonged to their family for years. He loved his family, but he needed to make his own way and be his own man.

"You've done enough traveling. Come on, and I'll drive you over to show you the shop." Jeremy gave his wife another quick kiss. "Call me if anything happens."

Grace shoved him toward the back door. "I'll be fine. Tate, we're glad you're here."

"Thanks. It's great to meet you." Tate followed Jeremy to a work van, slid inside, and waited for his cousin. "You did good. Grace is beautiful."

Jeremy cranked up the engine. "I definitely hit the jackpot."

"So, you really like living here in Crawdad Beach?"

"I do," Jeremy nodded as he drove away from the downtown area. "It's been better than I could have imagined. Plus, I don't have to worry about shoveling through snow every winter."

"Yeah, I get that. I do not miss the Chicago cold." Tate stared out the window as Jeremy crossed over unused railroad tracks, turned onto a gravel road, and slowed as he drove beside a large, white-block building.

"That's the main workshop," Jeremy pointed. He then parked in front of a big metal building behind the shop. "My great-uncle used this for additional storage. Aunt Helen said he hoped to try his hand at metalwork but never got around to it since he stayed so busy with other projects."

"Are you just saying that to get me to stay?" Tate stepped out of the van and followed his cousin.

"No, I think it's cool that you guys wanted to do the same thing." Jeremy unlocked the door, handed Tate the key, and ushered him inside.

Tate couldn't believe how nice it was. Although it wasn't new construction, the inside was in pristine condition. There wasn't even one stain on the concrete floor.

Jeremy took a piece of paper off an old wooden desk. "These are the specs on the building. It's 20'x40'14', with 14-gauge framing, a 10'x12' garage door, a 36'x80' walk-in door, and three 30'x36' windows. There's a small bathroom with a shower in the back."

"This is great. But, man, I can't take this from you. It's part of your inheritance. Let me at least pay you for the use of the building."

Jeremy tapped a finger on his chin. "Okay. It's yours for twenty-five dollars."

"You're kidding?"

"No joke," Jeremy said. "We don't need the money. Didn't you hear what we found at Knick Knacks?"

"The treasure?" Tate had heard the stories about what they'd found hiding in the old building. They'd kept it out of the news but not out of the family grapevine.

"Yep. We're good. I'm not using the building. I know Aunt Helen would love to see it put to use. Plus, if you buy it from me, it will help with my taxes."

Tate took his wallet out of his back pocket, grabbed the money, and handed it to Jeremy. "It's a deal."

Chapter 3

Brooke couldn't believe all the new businesses as she drove her car on Crawdad Beach's busy main street. The buildings that had been empty were now renovated and occupied. People filled the sidewalks, and most parking spaces were full. The sleepy little town had awakened.

She turned off the main drag and drove to Chester and Maybelline's house. Parking in their driveway, Brooke stopped her car. The house and yard were still well-maintained. Bright yellow and orange mums sat in pots on either side of the front door, welcoming anyone who stopped by.

With a groan, Brooke dropped her head to the steering wheel. Why had she come back? The Taylors gave her a home during high school, but even their kindness and love didn't help her feel settled. Thankfully, she was no longer a desperate girl willing to do anything to fit in with the popular crowd, but still, she'd always be the outcast.

Might as well get it over with and go see them. Brooke put on her jacket, took a deep breath, and exited her car. The damp air made her shiver as she walked to the front door. She still had a key to their house. Should she use it or ring the doorbell?

Would the Taylors even recognize her? After ten years, she'd changed. Besides being older, she'd lost weight and kept her once long, reddish-brown hair cut short. Her jeans were ripped, not in a fashionable way, and her shirt was one she'd worn for years. She pulled her jacket tighter as she stared at the doorknob.

She shouldn't have come here. Ten years ago, she'd taken the car they'd given her, drained the bank account they'd set up for her, and ran away. When she did, she texted them saying goodbye and thanked them for loving her but then discontinued all contact.

Brooke rubbed her forehead. She didn't deserve to be welcomed back. She'd ignored the Taylor's calls, texts, and emails for years. They'd kept her updated on their family and what was happening around Crawdad Beach. Brooke read them all but never responded. Why would they ever want to see her again?

The door flew open, and Maybelline threw her arms around Brooke, almost knocking her down. "You're home! Chester, she's home!"

He ran toward them and smushed them all together in a big hug. "Our baby is home! Thank God, our girl is home."

"We've missed you so much," Maybelline said through tears. "We have prayed for you every day, every night, asking God to keep you safe and bring you home. Thank you, God!"

Brooke didn't know whether to laugh or cry, so she did both. How could they welcome her so easily?

Her adoptive parents looked the same, just older, with

more lines on their faces. Maybelline still wore a bouffant hairdo, and Chester's hair was now all white.

Brooke pushed back, swiped tears from her face, and stared at her scuffed-up tennis shoes. She didn't deserve their affection. "I'm sorry. I'm so sorry. I should have stayed in touch."

Lifting Brooke's chin, Maybelline's kind, teary eyes gazed into hers. "No apology necessary. You're home. That's all that matters."

Chester nodded. "We love you, and that won't ever change. Come on in, and let's get you warmed up. Maybelline's got dinner ready. It's your favorite."

Brooke bit her lip to make it stop trembling. How did she know to make shrimp creole? Nobody on the planet could make that dish like her adopted mom.

"I just finished and made plenty." Maybelline put her arm around Booke and led her inside.

"Do you mind if I freshen up first?" She needed a few minutes to compose herself.

"Of course not. I'll set the table."

Even Chester had teary eyes. "Do you need me to get your bags out of the car?"

Brooke smiled through her watery vision. "Maybe after we eat."

"I'm glad you're home," Chester said. "Your room is ready. Every week, Maybelline changes the sheets and keeps everything clean. She kept all your belongings, boxed them up nice and neat, and placed them in your closet. We never stopped believing that we would see you again."

Unable to speak with a big lump of emotion clogging her throat, Brooke went down the hall toward the bathroom and stopped to peek into her old room. Her bedroom was now tastefully decorated in something similar to what she would have chosen for this stage of her life.

Scanning the room, Brooke gasped at a massive stack of presents sitting in one corner, some in birthday and others in Christmas wrapping.

"We saved them all for you." Maybelline came next to her. "You might want to exchange a few things, but I hope you enjoy seeing what we had chosen for you."

Brooke fisted a hand in front of her mouth as a sob tore loose. How could they still be so nice to her?

Maybelline's gentle arms came around her. "Oh, Brooke, we never stopped loving you. I don't know where you've been, what you've done, or what has happened, but our love for you will never change. We're so glad you're home."

Tate couldn't believe how great everything turned out. They'd gone to the town's law office to draw up papers, and the lawyer was already filing the deed to make the sale official. Tate had also filed for a business license. Jeremy and Grace had offered the use of their fold-out couch, but Tate didn't want to intrude, especially since a baby was coming. And sleeping on a sofa did not sound appealing.

Before the trip to Crawdad Beach, he'd sold the small travel trailer he'd used as he crisscrossed the country to work welding jobs. Some money from that sale went to savings; the rest went for a deposit to rent a place for six months. Since he didn't have any furniture, the fully furnished duplex in town was perfect.

Tate unloaded the equipment from his trailer into his new building. He'd been planning and saving for years, and now he finally had enough space to purchase a flat laser machine. Between that and his welding equipment, he could design, plan, and build to his heart's content.

He glanced around. How did he get so lucky? His parents would say it wasn't luck but God's blessing. He agreed. Tate sent a quick thank you prayer to God.

After what he'd done in the past, he sure didn't deserve any blessings from God. Yet, God had forgiven him. He just wished he could go back and fix what had happened.

Brooke lay in bed and stared at the ceiling of her old room. Dinner had been incredible as they sat around talking and laughing for hours as though she'd never been gone a day. Then Brooke had unwrapped ten years of birthday and Christmas presents. She couldn't believe they kept them all. Most gifts were from Chester and Maybelline, yet many were from their older children, her brothers and sisters. Even though they had already moved on with their lives before the

Taylors had adopted Brooke, they still welcomed her as though she'd grown up in their family.

Why had she waited so long to come back to Crawdad Beach? Brooke sent a quick text to update Fenton, then rolled over and closed her eyes.

Memories jolted her wide awake. While in high school, she'd attended the church's youth group. The girls had been sitting around talking about fun memories from their childhood when Brooke made the mistake of sharing something she thought was a decent memory. Instead, she was met with scrunched-up noses and looks of pity from the other girls.

Plus, she'd fallen for a handsome senior in high school when she was a sophomore. He told her she was pretty, made her feel special, and they started dating. She felt free with him and even told him about her parents and growing up in foster homes.

After dating for a few weeks, he took her to a nice restaurant and then drove to a secluded area. When things got out of hand, she'd shoved him away. There was no way she would be like her mother. Her date got mad, took her home, didn't get out of the car, didn't even kiss her goodnight, just sat there staring forward with his car idling while she went inside.

The next day, he told his friends she was the daughter of a prostitute. From that point forward, Brooke kept to herself what had happened in her childhood.

If only she could erase her past. And why couldn't she

wipe away that horrible night when she was away at college?

Her bedroom door creaked open, and a soft light spilled from the hallway as Maybelline entered. "Are you awake?"

"Yeah, come on in," Brooke said.

The mattress dipped as Maybelline sat beside her. "We're so glad you're home."

"I'm sorry I didn't stay in touch."

"The past is over, and it's a new day. Or, almost a new day," Maybelline said with a soft chuckle. Her hand gently brushed a stray hair out of Brooke's face. "I like your short hair."

"You're not mad that I cut it off?"

"Why would I be upset? The hairstyle makes your beautiful face and hazel eyes stand out even more."

Brooke puffed out a scoff. "Right." Maybe she was decent looking but beautiful? Not by a long shot.

"Oh, sweet girl. I wish. No, not just wish. I pray that you'll discover the beautiful person you are. Brooke, you're more than your birth heritage or what happened in the past. The God of the universe uniquely created you, loves you with an unfailing love, and has good plans for you."

She wanted to roll her eyes at Maybelline's religious, churchy comments but didn't want to hurt her feelings. "It would be nice to get into the good plan stage." She'd had enough of the bad stuff.

Maybelline gave Brooke a soft kiss on her forehead. "Get some sleep, and we'll see what God has planned in the morning."

"Would the morning come with some of your awesome homemade pancakes?"

Maybelline chuckled as she rose to her feet. "You bet. I love you, sweet girl. Sleep well."

"I love you, too." Brooke stared again at the ceiling as her bedroom door softly closed.

Being back in Crawdad Beach might be okay. But what would she do when her path crossed with people who knew her in high school? She'd been an absolute mess trying to fit in. She didn't drink, do drugs, or mess around, but she'd done stupid things to get attention to try to be with the popular crowd. All that did was make her even more of an outsider.

Brooke groaned and pulled the covers over her head.

Chapter 4

Restless to prove her worth, Brooke had already repaired her old bike, and then she fixed an old blender, a toaster, and a mixer. She'd found a box full of broken appliances in the garage, some of which she remembered from when she was in high school. She sat on the wooden stool in front of the workbench as she worked on an old wind-up alarm clock.

While in foster care, she tinkered with anything she could get her hands on. She couldn't fix her situation, so she fixed anything she could. Staying busy had kept her somewhat sane.

"Thought I'd find you here." Chester's knees creaked in protest as he knelt beside her.

"I can't believe you kept all these old things."

The corners of Chester's eyes crinkled with his smile. "I knew you would fix them. You've always had that gift. Thanks for doing that for us."

Brooke stared at her adopted dad. Although older, he was still in good shape. "How did you know I would come back? I didn't think I'd ever return." She still couldn't believe she'd actually done it, come back after what happened.

"We've been praying and believed God would bring you home." He made the statement without hesitation, like he knew all along that she'd return. "Brooke, you always have a home with us. We love you. Always have and always will."

"I don't deserve your kindness." Tears blurring her vision, Brooke looked away. "You wouldn't love me if you knew."

"Nonsense. Our love for you has never changed and won't change no matter what you've done or what has happened in your life." He placed a hand over his chest. "You live here in our hearts. There's not a thing you could tell us that would change our love for you." Chester stood and gently kissed the top of her head. "Come on inside. Maybelline has pancakes ready."

Trying not to cry, Brooke nodded. "I'll be there in a minute."

After Chester left, she rammed her palms into her eyes to keep the tears from falling. How could they still love her? If they knew what she'd done, they'd be so disappointed.

She didn't love herself. How could they?

Brooke shoved off the stool, stood, and mentally shook off her thoughts. She was so sick of her past dragging her down and tired of being emotional. She couldn't change anything that happened anyway.

Today was a new day with new opportunities. Brooke straightened her back. She wasn't the pudgy, insecure little girl anymore, and she would no longer let her past define her.

Brooke's shoulders drooped. The truth was that she was a twenty-eight-year-old, slender, insecure woman with a crummy past.

Shaking off that gloomy thought, she went to the dining

table and sat beside her adopted parents. After Chester prayed, Brooke told them she'd lived in Nashville.

"We didn't know you wanted to be a country singer," Chester said as he took a pancake and set it on his plate.

"I didn't. I can't carry a tune if my life depended on it. I figured I could find work there since it's such a busy place."

"Did you enjoy working in the shop?" Maybelline asked. "I can't imagine working on small engines or bikes. You've always had an amazing talent for fixing anything."

"I did enjoy working for Fenton. It was much better than waitressing or working in the bars." She shuddered at those unpleasant memories. "Fenton, the owner, let me help with all sorts of projects. Nothing was too big or small. He even let me handle his online advertising and taught me the accounting software he used. He's an amazing mentor and such a nice man. He and his wife really treated me well."

Maybelline gently laid her hand on Brooke's arm. "We are very grateful that God directed you somewhere safe. Fenton's shop sounds like it was made to order just for you."

"Yep, sounds like it." Chester gave Brooke a look like she was smart enough to be a brain surgeon. "You've always been good with your hands." He turned to Maybelline. "Brooke fixed all the old appliances we had stored in the garage."

"Oh, Brooke. Thank you so much. That's so sweet of you."

"You're welcome. I love doing stuff like that." Wait a minute, had she told them she worked in a small engine repair and bike shop?

Brooke took another bite of her adopted mom's special pancakes and narrowed her eyes as she surveyed them. Even when she was in high school, they seemed to know what was going on in her life. Were they that perceptive, or had they tracked her down? And could Maybelline be right that God directed her? Even when she'd been the one running?

"After breakfast, I'd love to take you to meet Jeremy, who owns Knick Knacks," Chester said. "He's the great-nephew of Helen Bounds. Jeremy has a workshop where he repairs and repurposes old furniture and even works on some antique lighting fixtures. Henry Doss and I help Jeremy out sometimes during the week. I'm sure he could use an extra set of hands if you want to do something like that. No pressure, though."

"There is definitely no pressure," Maybelline added. "But please visit the store. Jeremy married Grace Soloman, and I know Grace would love to see you. She asks about you all the time."

"Really? Grace was a good friend. It would be good to see her." Brooke readied her fork for another bite of pancake. Was she ready to face Grace and those who knew her before? And did she want to start working in Crawdad Beach?

Even though Chester and Maybelline made her feel welcome, living in the house again with them was a little strange now that she was older. Maybe she'd check out the loft apartments and see if they had an opening. Either way, Brooke would take it one day at a time before making long-term plans. She wasn't sure if she wanted to stay, but she couldn't think of anywhere else to go.

Tate ran his hand along the flat laser machine he'd had delivered this morning. The machine was used but in great shape and would cut, engrave, or mark metal, wood, or composite material. With his combined equipment, he could provide metal or steel fabrication. He could even make or repair wrought iron fences, iron handrails, and driveway gates, doing custom fabrication and any welding job needed. He couldn't wait to get started.

Last night, he had dinner at Jeremy and Grace's apartment above the antique store, and they brainstormed on items for Tate to fabricate and sell at Knick Knacks.

Sitting at the old wooden desk in the shop, Tate typed a list on his laptop. He'd make samples to display in his shop and small objects for the antique store. He also needed to get an appointment to meet with the local builder, Katherine Mitchell, who renovated many of the downtown buildings and houses in the area.

He also needed a website, social media exposure, business cards, and maybe even some flyers to help with advertising. He was only semi-proficient in those areas. Thankfully, Grace had offered to help him since she managed those things for their antique store.

First, he needed to drive to Doohickey's Hardware, pick up supplies, place an order for anything else he needed, and get started on his new business.

Tate closed his computer and grabbed his truck keys from his jeans pocket. Just one major problem: what would he call his business? He could use his name, Tate Tillman. Using his initials was not an option since neither TT Industries nor TOT Industries sounded professional. He locked up his shop and slid into his truck.

He could use Tate Tillman Enterprises. Maybe Metal Fabrication, Ironwork, and Welding by Tate Tillman. No, too dull and plain. He could be Iron Man Tate or Iron Man Tillman. Tate puffed up his chest as he started the engine. For once in his life, he'd love to be considered a hero, even if it was only on a business card.

Chapter 5

Brooke followed Chester inside Knick Knack's Antique Store. A high-pitched squeal nearly deafened her as her old friend, Grace, raced past Chester and threw her arms around Brooke. "You're home!

Brooke giggled at her old friend's surprising enthusiasm. "Yes, I'm here." Grateful and surprised to be greeted so warmly, Brooke nestled in her friend's arms. They met in the church youth group when Brooke first came to town. Although a few years older, Grace had taken Brooke under her wing and been a good friend.

"Maybelline called to let me know, and here you are!" Grace squeezed tighter.

"Best let the girl go so your baby doesn't get smushed," Chester said with a grin.

Grace stepped back and rubbed her belly. "Baby is dancing with joy."

Chester shook his head. "The poor kid is probably kicking to be let out."

"I hope not." Grace's eyes widened. "I'm not ready."

"Congratulations," Brooke pointed to her friend's swollen belly. "How far along are you?"

"Any day now." Grace's shoulders scrunched up as she

smiled. "We can't wait to see him or her. I've had ultrasounds, but we want to be surprised."

"You look great." Grace used to be shy, wore glasses, and kept her hair in a ponytail. Now, her big brown eyes were no longer hidden, and her hair fell free around her shoulders. She even seemed self-assured and happy.

"Aw, thank you," Grace's cheeks tinted pink. "You look wonderful, too. I love your short hair."

"Thanks. It's easier to take care of." Sometimes, she missed having long hair, but since she worked on machines and bikes, she didn't want to get tangled up in anything.

"I hope you're back to stay."

"I haven't decided what I'll do yet."

Chester cleared his throat. "We were hoping Jeremy might need a helper in his workshop."

"What a great idea," Grace said.

Brooke held up a hand. "I'm not sure if I'm staying. So, it might be temporary."

"What's all the excitement?" A tall, brown-haired, good-looking guy with a well-trimmed beard walked toward them.

Smiling wide, Grace grabbed his arm. "Jeremy, meet my good friend, Brooke."

He turned his blue-eyed gaze on her and smiled. "Nice to meet you."

Brooke shook his outstretched hand. "Nice to meet you, too." From the loving looks Grace and Jeremy gave one another, Brooke was happy for her friend, but her heart squeezed, watching something she probably would never have.

"Honey," Grace addressed her husband. "Brooke would like to help in your workshop."

"Brooke can fix anything," Chester said with a proud look. "You wouldn't believe how talented she is."

"We sure could use the extra help in the store and the shop." Jeremy turned to face Brooke. "Since that popular magazine featured Crawdad Beach, we've had more business than we can handle. We have money in the budget to hire someone. Since your dad and Grace speak so highly about you, we'd love to have you work with us."

She glanced at the hopeful expression on everyone's faces. Was she even staying in this town? Then again, she had nowhere else to go, and working would keep her busy. "Okay, it's a deal."

Grace squealed again. Chester shook Jeremy's hand. And Brooke wondered what she'd gotten herself into.

"Come on," Grace tugged on Brooke's arm. "I'll show you around the place."

With Grace chatting away about all they sold in the store, Brooke followed her friend as they weaved among the items. Grace then led her upstairs to their apartment. Brooke was surprised at how nice it was with hardwood floors, brick walls, exposed beamed ceilings, an open kitchen, and a fireplace on the back wall.

"This is great." Brooke would love to live in a place this nice.

"Thank you. We like it. But we've already bought a house

in town since we needed more space. Katerine Mitchell is finishing the remodel and should have the house ready before the baby comes. Do you remember Katherine? She's Henry Doss's daughter and is married to Michael Mitchell, the owner of Mitchell's Grocery. David and Tess are their kids. They're closer to our age."

Brooke nodded as she tried to remember who everyone was. She did remember that Henry Doss and his family had always been kind to her.

Grace sat on the couch and rubbed her stomach. "If all goes well, we move into the house in the next few days."

Brooke settled next to her. "I'll be glad to help when you move."

"Thank you. We can always use an extra pair of hands since I won't be very useful in my condition. So, I heard you were living in Nashville. Did you like it? What did you do while you were there? Sorry if I'm being too nosey."

"Nashville was nice, but it's growing like crazy. Traffic is getting worse by the minute. I worked in a small engine and bike repair business and lived in an apartment over the shop."

"That sounds perfect since you always liked fixing things."

"It was a good place to work. The owner and his wife were nice people and kind of watched over me."

"I'm so glad. I was worried about you. When Maybelline told me you'd left, I was heartbroken. Did your decision have to do with ... you know?"

Brooke sucked in a wobbly breath at the memory. Only

Grace knew part of what had happened. "Yeah, I couldn't face anyone."

"You didn't need to run." Grace's voice was gentle, caring.

"I did, too. It was my worst nightmare. The last thing on earth I ever wanted to be was like my mother." She had guy friends and numerous offers to go out on dates, but since that night, she'd turned everyone down. She couldn't risk being like her mother.

"You aren't *anything* like your mother. You got drunk and found yourself in a difficult situation. You made one mistake."

"Mistake? A mistake is putting salt in your coffee instead of sugar." Brooke shoved off the couch. Wishing she could squeeze out the heartache and horrible memory of what she'd done. "What happened was ... so much worse."

"I think you read too much into things." Grace struggled to her feet. "Maybe he didn't mean anything by it and was just trying to be nice."

Brooke crossed her arms over her chest. "I'm not misreading what happened. He seemed like a nice guy, but what do I know? I was so drunk or drugged that I could hardly stand. I can think of a million ways to be nice, like kissing me goodbye or apologizing, but doing that was the worst thing on earth he could have done. He must have thought I was a.." She choked on a sob, trying to escape. She couldn't say the word.

"I'm sorry, Brooke." Grace pulled her into a hug. "I'm so sorry."

Brooke stiffened. She didn't want to cry. But the tears wouldn't be held back.

"Grace," Jeremy's voice came from the stairway. "Can I borrow Brooke to show her the shop?"

"We'll be right down." Grace held her close. "You want me to go with you?"

"No, I'll be fine." Brooke pushed away, swiped the tears from her face, and straightened her back. She knew how to pretend to be okay. She'd done it all her life.

"Let's catch up later." Tears still ran down Grace's eyes. "I've been praying for you since you've been gone. I'm glad you're back."

"Thanks." Before she got emotional again, Brooke hurried down the stairs.

Tate worked on his new project. Katherine Mitchell had hired him on the spot to make decorative iron handrails for the porch steps of Jeremy and Grace's new house. Tate already loved living in Crawdad Beach. The people were friendly, Tiddlywinks Restaurant had great food, and Rolling in the Dough Bakery had the best muffins he'd ever eaten. What else could he need?

He tamped down the familiar ache rising in his chest. No matter how nice the town was, he still had no one to share his life with.

Chapter 6

"You like football?"

Grateful to be talking about a subject she enjoyed, Brooke grinned at Jeremy's surprised expression. "No, I *love* football. It's great watching athletes in action, seeing them call a play, and no matter how it turns out, they have to keep going, moving forward to the goal."

"That's a cool way to look at it."

"My boss, Fenton, was a former college football star. He and his buddies taught me about the game. It's like a chess match between offense and defense."

Jeremy chuckled as he pulled his work van in front of a big white building. "Sounds like you could teach me a few things. Until I got older, I was too short for basketball, too skinny for football, and too uncoordinated for soccer."

He opened the door of his workshop and showed her inside. "As you can see, we have lots of projects."

Although clean and well-maintained, the building was crowded with old furniture, antique lighting fixtures, saws, sanders, a paint section, a lathe, and almost every tool she'd ever wanted to use.

Brooke already loved the place. It reminded her of the big guy's shop on the home remodeling show. "This is wonderful. I can't wait to get started."

One of her foster families had allowed her to refinish old bedroom furniture to use in her room, and she'd loved learning another way to work with her hands.

"Great. I have a list of the current projects." Jeremy opened an old wooden file cabinet and handed her a manilla file folder full of scraps of paper. "Sorry, I don't have a better system."

Brooke thumbed through his handwritten notes and then glanced around to find the location of the items he'd started.

Jeremy tapped the file cabinet. "I've kept ideas in the second drawer. Cutouts from magazines, pictures from social media, whatever is trending, that we might be able to sell in the store. You're welcome to try your hand at pretty much anything."

She gave him a curious glance. "Besides handling the current projects, you're just going to set me free to design and work on whatever I want?"

"Sure. I'll be in and out when I'm not at the store. Chester and Henry Doss come in to help some days, which is always entertaining." Jeremy gave a light chuckle. "My Aunt Helen and Maybelline, along with Chester, wander the backroads for yard sales and anything we might be able to sell in the store." Jeremy handed her a key. "This is to the workshop. I'm looking forward to seeing your ideas."

"Thanks. I'm excited to get started."

"You can start tomorrow morning." Just keep track of your time. I'll pay you overtime if you work more than forty hours a week.

"Would you mind if I started today?" Brooke asked. "I can't wait to get going." The projects seemed to be calling her. Working in Fenton's place was wonderful, but this would be equally nice. She'd actually be getting paid again to do something she enjoyed with freedom to create in a workshop with every tool she'd ever want or need.

"That would be great," Jeremy said. "Since you probably want to wear work clothes, I'll drive you back to town. You can come back whenever you're ready."

"Won't take me long to change. Thanks for the opportunity, Jeremy."

"Are you kidding me? Thank you. Having you working with us takes a load off our shoulders. Especially with a baby coming."

Brooke followed Jeremy to his work van and slid inside.

He backed up the vehicle, stopped, and pointed to the big metal building behind the workshop. "My buddy and cousin, Tate Tillman, works back there. He's a great guy, so you don't need to worry. Tell you what, I'll swing down that way to introduce you."

Tate had already cut the wrought iron stock to the specified size, set them into a jig, and then welded all the components to form a strong bond.

Once finished, he used the grinder to make the welds nice

and smooth. After that, he took trisodium phosphate to remove any oil residue.

Tate opened the big garage door to let in fresh air and spray-painted the finished product. All that was left was to give them time to dry, and then he would deliver them to Katherine Mitchell to be installed.

Tate stepped outside and stretched his back. Spotting Jeremy's work van, he waved as the vehicle pulled beside him.

Jeremy's window rolled down. "Tate, I'd like you to meet Brooke Taylor. She's a good friend of Grace and will be helping us out in the workshop."

Tate smiled at the beautiful woman with short hair. "Nice to meet you."

Her gaze was a little wary as she nodded. "Likewise."

"See you around," Jeremy said.

Tate watched as they drove away. He might have to drop in the workshop occasionally to see if Brooke needed help. He chuckled as he went back inside. Crawdad Beach continued to get better every day.

Chapter 7

Dressed in work clothes, Brooke surveyed Jeremy's handwritten notes listing the projects to be completed for the antique store. Furniture needed to be repaired, stripped, and refinished or painted. Antique light fixtures needed rewiring and updating. The list continued with enough projects to keep her busy for the rest of her life. This was a dream job.

Plus, having a good-looking guy working in the next building was nice. Tate had blue eyes, brown hair, a short, almost military-style haircut, a close-cropped beard, a muscular body but not overly so, and probably stood around six feet. Not that she noticed. Brooke shook her head. She was *not* planning on dating anyone, but knowing someone would be around if she needed help was nice.

Brooke turned her attention to Jeremy's first item: repurposing an old three-drawer dresser into a bathroom vanity. He'd printed out a step-by-step process from a website and already made the top drawer into a false front, the next drawers he'd placed blocking to give internal support and put in new drawer slides, and he'd even cut out a hole for where the sink would go. Her job would be to refinish the piece to his specifications.

Since Jeremy had included a picture of what he wanted

the finished product to look like, she first needed to strip off the old varnish to prepare it for a modern, mid-century look. Fortunately, the dresser was so old that the varnish barely hung on the wood, so she wouldn't need a stripping agent.

Brooke crossed to where the sanding supplies were stored. Some sanders were newer models, while others looked antique. She selected one with a dust catcher, put on ear protection, and got to work.

The old layer of varnish disappeared under the vibration of the electric sander. As Brooke worked, the old wood looked new again. She turned off the sander and ran her hand along the smooth surface. If only she could remove her past as easily and start fresh.

Maybe this would be her chance. If she decided to stay, she could save enough money for her own place. In high school, she used to ride her bike to a small, beautiful house with a wrap-around porch two streets over from the Taylors. After work today, maybe she'd see if it was still standing.

What was she thinking? Brooke huffed out a breath. She couldn't make long-term plans. Just because Chester, Maybelline, and Grace were glad to see her didn't mean other people would be. No one wanted to be around the daughter of a prostitute. Even her loser of a dad didn't want her around. She should never have found him. It was better not knowing.

Brooke grabbed a piece of sandpaper and worked on the areas the sander couldn't reach. As a little girl, she used to imagine her father would come to her rescue and make everything right. But he never came.

Before Brooke sanded a hole in the wood, she stopped and leaned against the dresser. When she went away to college and watched all the girls with their fathers, she had searched to track down hers. Hoping he would be happy to see her, she found where he worked, drove three hours, and waited outside his business.

When he left for the day, she couldn't get the nerve up to say anything. Instead, she'd followed him to a bar, ordered a coke, and watched him flirt with women half his age. Sick of his behavior, she paid her bill.

As she got up to leave, he blocked her path. "Hey, good looking. Can I buy you a drink?"

"No." She shoved past him. He never wanted her, and she sure didn't want him.

He caught her arm and leaned closer. "I can show you a really good time."

Bile rising in her throat, she smacked him in the chest. "I'm your daughter!"

He stumbled back and stared at her like she was something he'd found on the bottom of his shoe. "I don't know who you are."

Brooke told him his mom's name.

He scoffed. "That tramp probably just named me as the father because she didn't know who he was."

That did it. Brooke hit him in his sorry face. Based on the blood spurting from his nose, she'd probably broken it. She groaned at the memory of the foul names he called her.

She really needed a punching bag. Brooke picked up the

sander and went to work on another piece of furniture. What happened with her dad was bad enough, but what happened next made her want to sand off her head.

"I hope you're hungry." Maybelline, carrying a covered dish, walked toward her. "I thought you might want something to eat."

Brooke tried to smile. "Thanks." She hadn't even noticed her come into the building.

Maybelline set the plate down on the workbench and pulled her into a hug. "Are you okay?"

"Yes," she lied.

"No, you're not." Maybelline pulled back, her compassionate gaze searching her eyes. "What happened? Do you not want to work here?"

"Yes, I want to work here. It's great." Brooke picked up a chisel and gouged out a piece of the workbench. "It's not that. I was just thinking about my dad."

"Oh, Brooke. I'm so sorry. You don't have to keep allowing the mistakes of your parents or your own mistakes to keep you from moving forward."

"Easy for you to say. You're not the daughter of a prostitute and probably haven't done anything bad in your life."

Maybelline scrunched up her nose as she shook her head. "If I had to list everything I did wrong, they would fill a 300-page book."

Brooke rolled her eyes at her adopted mom. "I doubt that."

"We've all messed up. Do you remember the story of Ruth in the Bible?" Maybelline asked.

"Yeah." If anyone had a problem, Maybelline had something from the Bible she shared. Brooke huffed out a breath before she recited what she remembered. "After Ruth's husband died, instead of going back to her people, she stayed with her mother-in-law, Naomi. They moved to Bethlehem, and Ruth wound up marrying a good guy named Boaz." The true-life account sounded more like a fairy tale to her.

"Did you know the name of Boaz's mother?"

"No, just that Boaz was a distant relative of Naomi. "

"Boaz's mother was Rahab."

Brooke shot Maybelline a look. "The prostitute in Jericho?"

"The one and the same."

"Good guy, Boaz was a prostitute's son?" Why didn't she know this before?

"Yes, and Rahab is even listed in the genealogy of Jesus Christ." Maybelline laid a gentle hand on Brooke's arm. "Never, *ever* think your background can hinder what God can do with you and through you." She picked up the dish and handed it to her. "Now, you need to eat and keep up your strength. I'll see you tonight.

"Yes, ma'am." Brooke stared at the food as Maybelline left. She wasn't in the mood to eat, but the tempting smell won out. No one could turn down Maybelline's cooking.

Brooke perched against the side of the workbench as she

ate. Maybe things worked out okay for Rahab. And Boaz was a good guy, so good things happened to him, but what about her and what she'd done?

Brooke gazed up at the ceiling. Where was the good ending for her story?

Chapter 8

After work, Brooke drove along the streets of Crawdad Beach. A surprising number of the houses had been renovated in the years since she'd been gone, and the rest were still well-maintained. The town had always taken pride in staying nice and tidy.

Spotting the house with the wrap-around-porch, Brooke stopped her car and leaned over the steering wheel. The big oak in front shaded the porch with wooden railings and square columns. The pretty flower beds Brooke remembered were gone as though grass and weeds had crept in, and no one took the time to keep it up. The yard hadn't been mowed or edged, and acorns dotted the brown grass. The house looked sad as if no one cared.

The widow lady used to take such pride in her flowers. Maybe she needed help with the yard work. Brooke turned off her car and stepped out. She could come by on the weekends if the lady needed help.

The woman in one of her foster families had been a garden club member and taught Brooke all about plants. But her son had taught her things she didn't want to know. She rubbed at the scar on the inside of her left arm, which she kept hidden by wearing long-sleeved shirts.

The wood creaked under Brooke's feet as she stepped onto the dusty porch. The paint was peeling on the columns, railing, wood siding, and the molding along the decorative glass panes. Stopping in front of the door, she squinted to read a weathered handwritten note behind the front door screen - *For inquiries, call this number.*

Inquiries? Did that mean the house was for sale? Brooke sucked in a breath, grabbed her cell phone out of her back jeans pocket, and took a picture of the note. What if she could buy her own place? Was that even possible? She had some money saved, but not much. Maybe that would be enough to put down to get a mortgage. Even if she could get a mortgage, did she really want to stay here?

Brooke tried to peek in the shutter-lined windows, but the curtains were closed. She stepped off the porch and walked around the property. The roof probably needed replacing and the siding painted, but from what she could tell, the foundation looked okay. The one-car garage at the end of the cracked asphalt driveway would be nice for storage. If she actually had anything to store.

She returned to her car and glanced at the other houses on the tree-lined street. A cute craftsman house was on one side, and a pink-brick house was on the other. A brick rambler two doors down was under renovation.

What would it be like to have her own home? She already loved her new job, and being back in Crawdad Beach so far had been good. Brooke started up her car and drove to the Taylors.

Yummy smells met Brooke as soon as she entered the house. She went to the kitchen and peered over Maybelline's shoulder. "You're making spaghetti? With your amazing meatballs?"

"I remembered you liked them." Maybelline grinned at her as she stirred the pot of sauce.

"Why are you still being so nice to me?"

"You're our daughter, and we love you."

Brooke leaned against the kitchen counter. "I'm the kid who ran off with your car and drained a bank account." She couldn't get rid of that guilt.

Maybelline set the wooden spoon and turned to her. "Oh, sweet girl, the car was yours. We gave it to you. And the money in the account was also yours. You didn't take anything that didn't belong to you."

"So, you're not mad about that?"

"Of course not." Maybelline pulled Brooke into a hug and patted her back. "We missed you terribly, but we are so glad you're home."

"Just like that?"

Maybelline smiled. "Just like that."

"Well, okay then." Brooke opened the silverware drawer. "I'll set the table."

"Thank you. Chester won't be in until later. He and Henry went out today looking for more old furniture for Knick Knacks. I think they drove to North Carolina."

Brooke took the silverware to the table. She'd carried the guilt of the car and money for ten years, and just like that, all was fine. Well, alrighty then, maybe it was time to settle down. She went back to the kitchen to get the plates. "What do you know about the house with the wrap-around porch?"

Maybelline grinned at her over her shoulder. "The one on Maple Street?"

"Yeah, I can't remember the name of the lady who lived there. Is she okay? The yard looked sad."

"It is sad. Mrs. Chapman died last year. Her daughter lives in Texas and doesn't get here often."

Brooke tried to act nonchalant. "Is she going to sell the house?"

"Yes," Maybelline said as she took breadsticks out of the oven and laid them on the stovetop. "Mrs. Chapman's daughter didn't want a sign in the yard, so it's been word of mouth. She hoped someone who lived here would buy it and fix it up."

"Really? Interesting."

One of Maybelline's eyebrows arched upward. "You thinking you might be interested?"

"I love that little house, but I probably don't have enough money to even think about it. Who would want to give me a loan? And I don't know if I'm staying." She had to add that disclaimer because what if things went sour?

"Oh." Maybelline brushed the breadsticks with melted butter and sprinkled garlic salt on top. "Have you checked your account lately?"

"My account? The one here? I didn't leave anything in it."

"I know. But, we've been putting money in every month

since you've been gone."

"What? Are you kidding me?" Brooke tried not to get too excited. Maybe it was only a few dollars a month.

"Chester would go into the bank every year and ensure you got a good interest rate. I thought we left you a message about that before."

Brooke stood there blinking. Obviously, she should have paid more attention to their messages and told them where she was. Oh, great, that's another thing she'd feel guilty about. Brooke smacked herself in the head. All she did was feel guilty. She shouldn't have even been born. Her mother and father never wanted her. The list of her wrongdoings just kept getting bigger and bigger. "I'm so stupid. I'm sorry. I'm sorry about everything."

Maybelline took Brooke's hands in hers. "You are not stupid. You are an intelligent, kind, beautiful young woman."

"Yeah, right. All I've done is screw up. And I keep replaying every wrong thing I've done as far back as I can remember. The angry words I said, the times I wasn't nice to other people, the idiot things I did for attention, and other stuff I never want to tell you about. I've asked God to forgive me, but they keep replaying over and over and over. I think I'm losing my mind. " She forced her hands to her side so she wouldn't yank on her hair.

Maybelline placed her hand on Brooke's forehead. "Just as I thought. You've got the Grrrrs."

"Well, I definitely feel like growling."

"That's what the Grrrs do to you. The Grrrs are guilt,

remorse, regret, replaying the negative, and shame. Brooke, we've all messed up. Every one of us has done something we regret. We've all sinned, and that's why we need a Savior. So, instead of the Grrrs, focus on God's grace. If you've asked God for forgiveness, the Bible tells us that when God forgives our sins, He removes them as far as the East is from the West. The replaying of your sins or silly things you've done isn't coming from God, so don't give them headspace. Kick them out and accept God's grace by giving yourself grace."

Brooke crossed her arms. "Well, that sounds too easy. Get rid of the Grrrs and replace them with grace." Brooke didn't mean to sound that sarcastic.

"It is easy, and it isn't." Maybelline handed her a breadstick.

Brooke took a bite and waited for another Biblical lecture.

Maybelline munched on a breadstick for a few minutes. "We all mess up and wish we could go back and fix things we did wrong or were embarrassing. Mistakes are part of life and part of our learning experience. None of us are born knowing how to do anything. We can't even walk without making some falls. Do you remember the first day you were learning to drive?"

"Yes, thanks for that reminder. I still feel guilty about that." Brooke tore a bite off of her breadstick. She had stepped on the gas instead of the brakes and ran over the garbage can.

Maybelline chuckled. "You don't need to feel guilty about

that. You learned the lesson, and I'm sure you haven't had any problems since. You turned out to be an excellent driver." Maybelline's kind eyes searched hers. "Brooke, none of us are perfect. We've all screwed up, and every one of us has sinned. God's mercies are new every morning, and He is a forgiving God. Embrace His grace."

Booke growled. "I've tried, and I don't know how!" She bit her lip to try and stop it from trembling. "Plus, you and God would never forgive me."

She stomped out of the kitchen and went outside to the back patio. The evening breeze chilled her, and she hugged her arms against her chest as she tried not to cry.

One of her foster mothers used to tell her to stop crying, or she'd give her something to cry about, and she meant it. Brooke rubbed her cheek as though she could still feel the sting of the slaps.

Collapsing on a lawn chair, Brooke ran her hands through her hair. What if some of the things she felt guilty about were just part of her learning experience? Maybe that would help filter a few things out, but not everything.

She deserved to feel guilty and ashamed for what she'd done that night after she met her so-called father.

"Brooke?" Maybelline called from the back door. "Would you come inside and eat? Please? Everything is ready."

Blast! If she didn't go inside and eat, she'd feel guilty that Maybelline had made a nice meal for her.

Brooke shoved out of the chair. She could fix appliances, small engines, restore furniture, and do a zillion things with her hands, but she didn't know how to fix her messed-up head.

Tate didn't mean to watch. He was sitting in his screened-in porch with his feet propped up, enjoying the evening, when he noticed Brooke step out of the house behind him. Why was she so upset?

He might have walked over and checked on her if he knew her better. He hated to see anyone hurting. But he needed to be careful. The last time he'd intervened to try and help someone, he'd made a mess of things for both of them.

Tate got to his feet and went inside.

Chapter 9

Brooke walked along the quiet beach as the sun peeked over the eastern horizon. The ocean breeze made her shiver, and she pulled her jacket tighter. She'd spent the entire night thinking about everything she'd ever done wrong, so she'd driven here to sort things out.

A seagull rode the air currents above her. She glanced up at the bird. "Sorry, I don't have anything for you." She didn't have anything to give anyone.

Maybelline had been her sweet self last night, reminding Brooke of the people in the Bible who had done terrible things yet had been forgiven by God and used in mighty ways. David had been an adulterer with Bathsheba and even had her husband killed, yet God used David and said he was a man after God's heart. Moses had killed a man. Noah got drunk.

Not anybody was perfect other than Jesus Christ. The one account that got to Brooke was about the woman who came into the Pharisee's house where Jesus was reclining at a table. The woman had been a known sinner, yet she wept at Jesus's feet, anointing them with her alabaster jar of perfume, wiping His feet with the hair of her head, and kissing His feet. Jesus told the woman her sins had been forgiven, that her faith had saved her, and to go in peace.

Would Jesus do that for her? She was a sinful woman—the daughter of a prostitute. She was so tired of feeling guilty and ashamed, so tired of being trapped in the Grrrs.

Was there any hope for her? Brooke gazed upward. "I sure could use some help down here." Nothing changed. The waves continued to lap the shoreline. With a heavy sigh, Brooke turned to go back home.

A white-haired woman wearing a long white coat walked toward her and stopped. "Good morning, Brooke." Her voice was kind, gentle, and smooth.

"Good morning." Brooke tilted her head as she tried to figure out how the lady knew her. The woman seemed older, but her skin was smooth as if she'd never had a worry in the world. Brooke felt drawn to the woman as though she were a close friend, someone she'd known for years. Maybe she was somebody from Crawdad Beach.

"God loves you." The woman's intense but kind blue eyes seemed to look into Brooke's very soul.

"Okay, thanks." What was she supposed to say?

"I knew your mother."

Gooseflesh rose on Brooke's arms. "You knew her?"

"Yes. Your mother always loved you, but she had a hard time believing that God could love her. I want you to know before your mom died, she gave Jesus Christ her heart, and He gave her His."

Brooke stared at the woman. How did she know?

The woman handed Brooke a closed oyster shell and tapped it. "Accept God's grace. Leave the past behind, and open each new day to see what God has planned."

Brooke pried the shell open. Inside sat a beautiful shimmering pearl.

She gasped and released a surprised puff of air. "Thank you so much."

She looked up, and the woman was gone. Brooke turned every which way, scanning the beach, but she was nowhere in sight.

Chapter 10

Accept God's grace. Leave the past behind and open each new day to see what God has planned.

The woman's words at the beach ran through Brooke's mind as she drove back to Crawdad Beach.

Accept God's grace. Could it be that easy? Could God, *would* God, really erase her past sins and cover her with His grace?

She'd officially accepted Christ as her Savior when she was seventeen and attended church every week while she lived with the Taylors. Then, when she lived in Nashville, she used to sit on the stairs of her apartment so she could listen as Fenton's friends studied the Bible together. Brooke had even attended church with Fenton's family, but still, she felt like she'd drifted away from God.

If only she'd stayed close, maybe her life would look different. Would God welcome her back as easily as Maybelline and Chester had?

Brooke parked her car and stepped out at the workshop. Tate honked his truck horn as he drove past. She waved, entered the building, and flipped on the lights. Brooke gently laid the oyster shell the mystery woman had given her on the bench and examined the pearl under the workbench light.

The pearl looked real. Brooke rubbed it against her teeth. Sure enough, it felt a little gritty, not smooth like an imitation. She opened her phone and did an internet search to find out how much a pearl like this might be worth.

Whoa!

If what she read was true, the woman had given her something worth a lot of money. Why? And just who was that woman? Was she an angel? And if she was, did things like that really happen today?

What was that story in the Bible about some man finding a valuable pearl? Brooke searched the internet and found the verse in Matthew. Jesus said that the kingdom of heaven is like a merchant looking for fine pearls, and when he found one of great value, he sold all that he had and bought it.

Brooke laid the pearl back in the shell and leaned down to study it again. Why was she given it without her even having to pay? She didn't have to do anything; it was just given to her.

Accept God's grace.

The hair on Brooke's arms raised, almost like standing at attention. She'd heard from Maybelline and others plenty of times that God's grace is freely given, and all she had to do was accept and receive it. Is that why the woman gave her the pearl?

Brooke looked up at the ceiling. Should she pray? What was she supposed to say? "Hi, God, it's me. Brooke Taylor." That didn't seem right. Maybe she needed to be more formal.

She bowed her head. "Hello, God. Heavenly Father. I'm

sorry I haven't talked to you in a long time. I've been pretty embarrassed about a few things. Which I know you know. I'm sorry. Would you please forgive me? I sure do need your grace." Brooke squeezed her eyes shut as the long list of things she'd done wrong came to mind.

Brooke groaned as she looked back at the ceiling. "Yeah, it's all those things. I'm really sorry for every one of them and even some I probably don't remember. Please forgive me." She swallowed hard as her tears fell. Maybe she needed to say something else.

"I think the word in the Bible says I need to repent. So, I do repent." Sniffling, Brooke swiped away her tears. "I know some of the bad things, the sins I've committed; I've already asked you for forgiveness. But this time, I want to be sure. I need to know that you've really forgiven me."

Tears running down her cheeks, Brooke fell to her knees. "Please, God, please forgive me. I've disobeyed. I've run from you. I've done things that I shouldn't. I've sinned. I repent. I need your grace. Please, God, forgive me. I want to come back to you."

Sobs wracked her shoulders as she cried for all she'd done wrong, and she cried for the wasted years away from God and being away from the loving adopted parents God had given her.

As she cried, she felt like a warm hand laid on her shoulder. She glanced behind her, but she was alone. She sucked in a breath. Was God telling her she was forgiven? Peace enveloped and wrapped around her and in her. "Thank you, God. Thank you."

Brooke stayed on the floor kneeling, loving the feeling of the nearness of being with God, being forgiven, and accepting God's grace.

If what the woman or angel said on the beach was true, that would mean Brooke would get to see her mom again, and she'd be healed and whole and happy.

Through her tears, Brooke puffed out a surprised laugh. "Thank you, God!"

Chapter 11

"I tell you, Henry, it was at least three feet long," Chester said as he entered the workshop from the back door.

Brooke got to her feet, wiped her eyes, and picked up the sander.

"Now, Chester, that's a stretch, and you know it." Henry Doss grinned as he followed behind. "That fish couldn't have been more than eighteen inches."

She chuckled as the men bantered back and forth. Henry and Chester were best friends and fishing buddies.

"Hey, sweet girl." Chester held up a brown paper sack. "Maybelline was worried you ran out this morning without breakfast. She made you some cinnamon rolls."

Brooke's mouth watered at the delicious aroma as she accepted the gracious offering. "Thank you so much."

"Welcome home." Henry was one of the sweetest men she knew. He gave her a grandfatherly hug. "We've missed you." Even though it was winter, he still smelled of spring soap and sunshine.

"I'm glad to be back."

Chester leaned over the oyster shell. "What have you found?" He motioned his friend over. "Check this out."

Henry whistled. "That's a beauty. Where did you get

this?"

Brooke took out a cinnamon roll. "I didn't find the shell or the pearl. When I was at the beach early this morning, a woman gave it to me." Happy goosebumps pebbled on her arms at the thought.

Both men's eyebrows rose to their white hairlines.

"Gave it to you?" Chester carefully picked up the pearl. "If this is real, it could be worth a fortune."

"I don't believe it's imitation," Brooke said. She took a bite of the delicious treat as she remembered her time with the woman and with God.

"You said a woman gave it to you?" Henry's radiant blue eyes crinkled with his smile.

Brooke swallowed. "Well, I *think* she was a woman."

Chester's head jerked her way. "You think?" He stepped closer and looked her over. "Something's different about you." He laid his hand on his chest. "Oh, my goodness. You've had an encounter!"

Henry nodded. "I see it too."

"God got you home, didn't He?" Chester danced a little jig.

Brooke giggled as tears rushed to her eyes. "I guess He did. I haven't ever felt this free." She felt clean and light, as though nothing was pressing down on her shoulders anymore.

Both men surrounded her and gave her the biggest hug she'd ever had as they praised and thanked Jesus.

"Best let the girl go so she can breathe," Chester said as she released her and wiped his teary eyes. "This has to be the best day ever. I've got to get home and tell Maybelline. She was up early this morning praying for you, telling me something was happening. I tell ya, that woman has a hotline to God."

Henry gave Brooke one more big squeeze. "I'm so happy for you." He leaned closer to whisper in her ear. "Whenever you're ready, I would love to hear about the angel who gave you the pearl."

Brooke kissed his sweet cheek. "I'll do that."

"Oh, wait." Chester snapped his fingers. "I forgot. Before we go, we have furniture and all kinds of items to be fixed and readied for the store. Finish your breakfast, and Henry and I will unload everything."

Through his open garage door, Tate could hear two older gentlemen straining to remove a big armoire off the back of a pickup truck.

Tate shut down his equipment and walked toward the men. "Can I give you guys a hand?"

"That's mighty fine of you. Thank you." One of the white-haired gentlemen held out his hand. "I'm Chester Taylor, and this is Henry Doss."

Tate shook both men's hands. "I'm Tate Tillman. Pleased to meet you both."

"You're Jeremy's cousin, right?" Henry asked. "He

mentioned you do welding and metalwork."

"That's right. He sold me the building that I'm using for my business. I've been working for years. First time I've had my own shop, though."

Henry smiled. "We're glad to have you in town."

"He lives behind us in the Bowman duplex," Chester said. "He's not married, either, and I heard he's a Christian."

Henry grinned. "Is that right?"

Tate tried not to laugh. "I am not married, I am a Christian, not perfect, and I am *not* looking for a woman."

Both men chuckled as they gave him sly grins.

What were they thinking? And just who would they want him to meet? Trying to ignore their hopeful stares, Tate positioned himself to help get the big piece of furniture off the truck.

Using every muscle in his body and then some he didn't realize he had, Tate struggled to move the mammoth piece. After more moaning and groaning than he'd heard in years, most of which came from him, they successfully placed the armoire inside the building.

Tate leaned over and tried to catch his breath. "How did you guys get this on the truck in the first place?"

"Well," Chester's smile looked sheepish. "The football team practicing in the field next to the house where we picked up the furniture might have helped a little."

Brooke walked toward them. "You should have told me you needed an extra hand."

Tate stood straight and tried not to act as sore as he was.

Up close, she was even prettier. "Hey." So much for making a suave comment.

Brooke's head tilted just a touch. "Hey." A tiny bit of a smile appeared as she looked at him. "I see they roped you into helping."

"He volunteered," Chester said with a big smile. He's a strong guy. Nice, too. Christian. Single." He wiggled his eyebrows.

She stood there a minute, just eyeing Tate. "Good to know."

Tate tried not to stare as she walked away, but something about her seemed familiar. Either way, he wouldn't mind getting to know her better.

Chapter 12

Brooke got back to work. As nice as it was knowing Tate was a good guy, she just got her life right with God; the last thing she needed was to think about a man. She needed to stay focused on work, stay out of trouble, save her money, and hopefully, someday, she could get her own place.

Crying and laughing, Maybelline rushed toward her. "Chester called me." She hugged and squeezed Brooke. "I'm so happy for you. Thank you, Jesus! Thank you, thank you!"

Brooke snuggled in Maybelline's arms. "Thanks, Mom. It's good to be home."

Maybelline gasped, her eyes wide and filled with tears as she leaned back. "You called me mom."

Brooke chuckled. "I guess I did." Why hadn't she said that sooner? Maybelline was more of a mom than her birth mother ever had been. What the woman, or lady angel, on the beach shared, had given Brooke a release to move forward. Her birth mother had made a mess of her life, but she was okay now and safe forever in heaven. And for the first time, Brooke felt she'd be okay, too.

Another of Maybelline's hugs enveloped her. "Oh, honey. Thank you. I love you so much."

"I love you, too. Thanks for being a great mom."

Maybelline stepped back and wiped her eyes. "Thank you, sweet girl. I'm so glad God brought you to us."

Remembering what a mess she was when she first came to live with the Taylors, Brooke scrunched up her nose. "No regrets?"

"Not one regret. Not ever. We knew the moment we saw you that God had given us the gift of you."

"Gift?" Brooke scoffed. "More like a stink bomb."

"Oh, honey, you've always been too hard on yourself. You had a rough childhood and were doing the best you knew how."

"Thanks for being a safe place." Some of her foster families had been nice and decent, others not nice or decent, but the Taylors had always been good to her, giving her a safe and loving home.

"We love you," Maybelline laid her gentle hand on Brooke's cheek. "Don't ever forget that." She clasped her hands in front of her and grinned. "Speaking of houses. I hope you don't mind, but I placed a call to find out how much the daughter wanted for her mom's house."

"The house I asked about?"

"Yes. When I told her our daughter was interested in buying it, she was excited and wants to talk to you. I think she's more interested in finding someone who will love the house like her mom did than making a big profit."

Brooke tried to temper her excitement. "That would be amazing. But I only have a few thousand dollars saved." She wasn't even sure how much the house was or how much down payment would be needed. But it was probably more than she had.

Maybelline's eyes crinkled with her smile. "Have you not checked the account we gave you?"

Brooke looked away. "No. I forgot."

"Well, since we're cosigners," Maybelline said. "I checked the account last night. It's now worth $18,000.00."

"What!" Brooke steadied herself against the workbench. "That's amazing. How is that even possible?"

"We've been making monthly deposits since you left."

"Why? I ran off and didn't talk to you. Why are you so nice to me?" Brooke stared at the pitted and stained workbench. What a mess she'd made of her life. "I would have written me off."

"You're our daughter, and we love you. Nothing changes that."

"So that money is just waiting for me?"

Maybelline grinned and nodded.

"Really? That would give me a great down payment, but it might not help me get a loan. I love my job, but I'm not earning a big salary."

"Don't you worry about that for a moment. I have no doubt you could get whatever you need if you want to buy the house."

"Is all this good stuff happening because I became a Christian?"

"Oh, goodness, no." Maybelline laughed. "Becoming a Christian is the best thing you can do for all eternity, but it doesn't mean you're guaranteed an easy life. The day I became a Christian, my car was hit by a drunk driver, my best friend stopped talking to me, and the guy I was dating dropped me like a hot potato."

Brooke's mouth dropped open as she stared at her mom. "Chester dropped you?"

"It wasn't Chester." Maybelline's cheeks tinted pink. "It was who I dated before. Brooke, I wasn't always living right. Some people called me a wild thing."

"You?" Brooke tried not to laugh, but the idea of Maybelline being wild was too much. "I always figured you walked the straight and narrow from the day you were born."

"Hardly," Maybelline grimaced. "Let me just say I'm grateful I was a teenager before social media existed. The nice thing is that when Jesus changes us, He does a wonderful job with the changing. Remember, the Bible says that if anyone is in Christ, they become a new creation. The old is gone."

Maybelline hugged her again. "I'll be at the library today if you need anything. It's my day to volunteer, so I had better get moving." She walked away, turned, and hurried back. "I almost forgot to give you the phone number to call about the house." She handed her a piece of paper with the lady's name and number. "Give her a call and make sure you tell her you're our daughter."

"Thanks, mom." It felt great saying that as she watched her hurry out the door.

Brooke placed the paper in her back jeans pocket and glanced around the shop. Like the furniture being remade and repurposed, would God give her a new start on life? Would the old Brooke 1.0 become the new, improved creation of Brooke 2.0?

Would she really be able to buy a home of her own? She looked up at the ceiling, smiled, and whispered a prayer of thanks.

Time to get to work. Brooke checked Jeremy's list and studied the picture he'd printed. Today's project would be to convert an upright four-drawer dresser to resemble a stack of vintage luggage. Brooke chuckled at the fun idea, which gave her a great visual of God remaking her.

She sanded off what little was left of the original dresser finish and cleaned up the area. She then removed the drawers and stained the sides in a dark walnut color. Leaving the top drawer bare, she stained the second one in a light oak and painted the third a creamy white using an antique glaze to make it look older and more distressed. The last drawer, she stained a reddish brown.

While everything dried, she took three of the worst-looking, non-salvageable pieces of luggage and removed the handles, latches, pulls, belts, decorative items, and any leather or vinyl that could be salvaged.

To make the top dresser drawer resemble a vintage piece of luggage, Brooke glued plaid brown vinyl from a soft-sided suitcase she'd salvaged and used a brown leather handle as the drawer pull. She placed two buckle straps on the second drawer on either side of a coordinated handle. The third drawer, Brooke used an old handle and rusty latches.

The last drawer, she placed a black plastic pull in the center and metal latches on either side of that. Brooke stepped back and admired her work. It did look like a stack of vintage suitcases.

She couldn't wait to see what Jeremy and Grace thought of the finished product. Brooke checked the time. How did it get so late in the day? She didn't even notice she'd worked through lunch.

Since she still had an hour before she planned on leaving, she checked the list to see if there was a small project to work on before she went home. Jeremy's list showed he wanted another piece of antique luggage to be repurposed into a nightstand, using hairpin legs as the base. She could do that, take the old and make it look new.

Brooke rummaged through the luggage, took out the best-looking piece, laid it on the workbench, and thoroughly cleaned the inside. While she worked, she prayed God would create in her a clean heart. Once finished, the old suitcase didn't even smell musty. Brooke polished it with a leather cleaner to make it look shiny and new. The final step was to find the hairpin legs. Brooke looked through Jeremy's metal items and found four.

Unfortunately, one was broken at the top. Brooke texted Jeremy, asking what he wanted her to do. He replied she should see if Tate could make the repair.

Brooke checked her clothes. She looked messy after all the sanding and painting she'd done today. But since she was not looking to attract a man, she had nothing to worry about.

She'd just walk over and ask Tate for his help.

But before she did, she'd wash up and make sure she was at least somewhat presentable.

Chapter 13

Brooke didn't want to interrupt Tate, and there was no way he could see her through his welding mask. Standing just inside the open garage door of his building, Brooke watched him welding.

There was something very satisfying about seeing someone work with their hands. Fenton used to tell her that God blessed each of us with gifts, callings, and talents, and she should be proud of her work. Fenton's favorite Bible account in Exodus 31 was about a man named Bezalel, who God filled with wisdom, understanding, and knowledge in all kinds of craftsmanship. Fenton even had a plaque in his shop with Colossians 3:23: *Whatever you do, do your work heartily, as for the Lord rather than for men,*

Tate stopped, flipped up his hood, turned off his welding equipment, and stowed his torch.

"Hey," Brooke called out as she walked toward him.

"Hey, back at you." He smiled as he took off his helmet. "Welcome to my shop."

"Thanks. What are you working on? It looks nice."

"This is the first section of an outside porch railing. Since I did the first house here in town, I have three orders from people wanting to update their front porches." Tate motioned with his chin toward Brooke. "What have you got there?"

"Sorry to bother you, but Jeremy said you should be able to fix this." She held up the broken hairpin leg. "It probably just needs a quick spot weld."

"You think so, huh?' Tate grinned as he took it from her and studied it for a moment. "Looks like you're right. Just give me a minute, and I'll get it done for you."

After he finished, he laid it on one of his workbenches. "Best let it cool for a minute. So, did you grow up in Crawdad Beach?"

"No, I lived all over." There was no way she wanted to share anything too personal. "How about you? Where did you grow up?"

Tate's blue-eyed gaze met hers. "Chicago area."

"Sounds cold. How did you get here?"

"My cousin, Jeremy, invited me. I'd been on the road for several years working as a welder around the country."

She gave him a sly grin. "Gypsy welder, huh?"

"I guess that's one way to put it. I had a travel trailer I used, or sometimes I'd stay in a hotel."

"Did you enjoy traveling?"

"Yes and no. I got to see places I'd always wanted to visit, but moving from place to place gets lonely after a while."

"I know that feeling." She'd moved enough that she was ready to stay in one place. At Tate's curious glance, Brooke grabbed the hairpin leg. "Thanks. I better get back to work."

"Right. Come by anytime."

"Thanks." Brooke grinned his way. "My door's always

open, too."

Tate smiled. "I'll remember that."

Brooke hurried back to the workshop and laid the hairpin legs on the workbench. She didn't need to get drawn in by a nice, handsome, blue-eyed guy. God gave her a new life, and she couldn't mess it up. She needed to walk the straight and narrow, even if that meant being alone.

Then again, Maybelline said she'd been wild before she became a Christian, and God gave her Chester as a husband. So, did that mean her life could be shared with someone?

Brooke groaned. With her past, how could she ever be with someone nice like Tate? Ugh. She needed to get back to work and stop worrying about stuff. She didn't want to get trapped in the Grrrs again.

Her phone signaled an incoming text. Brooke grinned as she read the message. Grace asked if she could stop by around six this evening to help with packing up their apartment.

Brooke sent a quick that she'd love to. Her pregnant friend probably needed all the help she could get. Thankfully, she'd have enough time to run home, take a quick shower, and grab a bite to eat. The nightstand project would have to wait.

Tate couldn't believe his cousin had actually bought a house and had a baby on the way. He pulled his truck behind

Knick Knacks and parked beside a rental moving van. He exited his truck, walked through the open back door, and went up the stairs to the apartment.

"Coming through." Jeremy and one of the biggest guys Tate had ever seen were carrying a couch down the steps toward him. He moved aside to let them pass.

Jeremy motioned with his chin. "Tate, this is Valentino. Valentino, this is my cousin, Tate."

"Nice to meet you." Valentino held the couch with one hand as though holding a feather and held his other toward Tate. Valentino looked like the hero in an action movie.

"Nice to meet you, too." Tate shook the man's massive hand.

"Grab any of the furniture you can carry," Jeremy said as they disappeared down the stairway.

Tate glanced around to see what he could carry on his own. In the kitchen area, Grace and Brooke were talking and laughing as they loaded boxes. He stood, enjoying the view. Brooke looked so familiar, but he couldn't figure out where they could have met.

Hearing someone coming up the stairs, Tate hurried to pick up the coffee table. A crash from the kitchen jolted his attention.

He rushed into the kitchen. A broken plate and a puddle of water were at Grace's feet as she leaned over and groaned. Gasping, she looked wide-eyed at Brooke. "I think the baby is coming."

Chapter 14

"**B**oil the water! Grab some towels!" Jeremy yelled as he ran around them.

Grace smacked him on the chest. "I am *not* having a baby here! Get me to the hospital." She leaned over again and groaned, then started doing that pregnant breathing thing.

Brooke tried to act calm. "It's okay. I heard first babies take longer."

Grace groaned again. "Tell that to the baby."

All the men stood, pale and wide-eyed, like their feet were stuck to the floor.

Brooke waved her hands. "Get Grace down the stairs and in the car! She needs to get to the hospital. Now!"

The guys jolted and bumped into one another. Good grief. What was wrong with them? "Jeremy, get Grace's go bag." He nodded and ran off.

Grace puffed breaths out as she pointed to her purse. "Get my cell and call Paige. She's one of the docs here in town."

Brooke took in some calming breaths and placed the call. Thankfully, Paige answered on the first ring and said she was coming. "She's on her way."

"Okay." Grace puffed again. "Let's get going."

Jeremy, a bag across his shoulders, came alongside. "I've got you. It's going to be okay." His words did not match his worried expression. "I called Aunt Helen. She's on her way."

Grace grabbed Brooke's arm. "You're with me."

Praying the doc named Paige would show up soon, Brooke followed behind.

"What can I do?" Tate whispered.

"I don't know. Maybe keep moving their belongings since they rented a truck."

"Good plan. I'll get the house key." Tate ran to Jeremy.

Brooke helped Grace into the SUV. "You're going to do great."

Carrying a black leather bag, a nice-looking, dark-haired woman about their age ran toward them. "I'm here."

"Paige!" Grace cried. "Thank you for coming."

"Do you need me to drive?" Paige asked Jeremy.

He looked like he was about to pass out. "No. Yes. I don't know."

"Give me the keys," Paige calmly said. "You sit next to your wife."

"Don't leave without me!" A woman with short silver hair hurried toward them and jumped in the back seat beside Jeremy. Brooke grinned when she realized who it was. Helen wasn't just Jeremy's great-aunt; she practically raised Grace after her mom died.

Grace smiled through her breathing. "Oh, Helen, thank you for coming."

"Are you crazy? I wouldn't miss being with you for

anything." Helen's gaze turned to Brooke. "I'm so glad you're back!"

Brooke chuckled. "It's good to be back." She leaned down to where Grace sat doing her breathing. "Since they're here, I'll stay and help pack up, okay? I'll come check on you later, okay?" At Grace's nod, she closed the car door.

As Brooke watched them drive away, she dialed Maybelline and told her what was happening. With a relieved sigh, Brooke placed her cell phone in her back jeans pocket.

"You okay?" Tate asked.

"Yeah, how about you?"

He grimaced. "I've never been involved in that kind of thing before. I know nothing about baby birthing." Tate shuddered. "But I can pray everything goes okay."

Valentino came next to them. "Prayer is the best thing. Hopefully, we will hear good news soon. Shall we continue with the move?"

"Let's do it." Brooke nodded at the man called The Eliminator. The Taylors had told her Valentino eliminated problems. One problem they had right now was getting the apartment cleaned out and the house ready before Jeremy and Grace brought home their baby. Thankfully, the couple had already boxed up their personal items.

Brooke followed Valentino and Tate up the stairs and returned to the kitchen to finish while the guys moved the furniture.

Maybelline hurried toward her. "I sent a text to the CBPT. I mean, the Crawdad Beach Prayer Team. Help is on the way.

Within thirty minutes, the apartment was crawling with help. Practically everyone Brooke knew in town came along with new people she hadn't met before. She'd never received that many hugs in her life.

They greeted her with affection and love, and not one person looked at her sideways or seemed to hold it against her that she'd run away. Brooke blinked hard to keep her tears from falling. Why hadn't she come back to Crawdad Beach sooner?

By ten o'clock, the apartment was empty and cleaned from top to bottom, the new house was set up for Jeremy and Grace, and the nursery was decorated and ready to welcome the new baby.

As people left, Brooke leaned against the nursery's door frame. What would it be like to be married, have a home, and have a baby? Was something like that possible for her? Probably not. No one would want her as a wife or a mother.

Maybelline nudged her. "Grace and Jeremy will be great parents."

"They will." Brooke rubbed at her scar. "Sometimes, I wish I could have that, but no one needs someone who's broken. God might have given me a new life, but I still have shattered pieces. Lots of mess to be cleaned up."

"Oh, sweet girl. In some ways, we're all broken. Life messes with us all. God promises that He heals the brokenhearted. Many hearts have been broken, wounded, and shattered. God also binds wounds, healing pain, and comforting sorrow. The key is to let God do the healing and binding. You don't have to hold on to your wounds and what happened in the past. Take them to God, the Great Physician."

She should have known she'd get a Bible lecture. Brooke glanced at Maybelline. "Easier said than done."

"You're right. It is. But, so very worth the effort. To step into the future, you've got to turn away from the past."

The sound of footsteps coming down the hallway turned their attention.

Tate held up his keys as he walked toward them. "If you think everything is ready, I'll lock up for the night. Chester's outside waiting."

"I think we're finished," Maybelline answered. "Brooke, you want to walk home with us?"

"I'll walk her home," Tate said. A red tint rushed to his neck. "I mean, I just live behind your house, and it would be no trouble."

With a knowing grin, Maybelline patted his arm. "Thank you for walking our sweet daughter home. That's very nice of you."

Tate dipped his head. "My pleasure, ma'am."

As Maybelline walked away, heat rose to Brooke's cheeks, and her lips gave way to a smile. She'd never had an offer from a man to walk her home, especially not a handsome, kind, strong man.

Oh, good grief. She was getting mushy. Brooke corralled her thoughts as she followed Tate outside and waited for him to lock the door.

During the move, she'd watched Tate while he worked and how he graciously interacted with other people. There was something kind and gentle about him that made her feel comfortable. Maybe she'd found a friend.

God forgave her, but could he heal all her broken parts? Even if she did, with all the things she'd done wrong, she was too unworthy of anything more than friendship.

Chapter 15

Every muscle in his body was sore, but he hadn't been this happy in years. Helping other people was like taking a B12 shot with a heavy dose of satisfaction. Tate finished locking the door to Jeremy and Grace's new house and turned to Brooke. She was leaning against the porch railing, gazing in the distance.

Tate stepped beside her. "You okay?"

"Yeah." Brooke smiled, and a slight dimple appeared on her cheek. "It's been a great day. I love helping people."

"I was just thinking the same thing."

She cast a look over her shoulder. "See that white house down the street? The lady that used to live there grew the prettiest flowers and kept her yard like something you'd see in a gardening magazine. She's gone now, and the house and yard look so sad. If I can save enough money, I'd love to buy it someday."

"I'm sure your parents would be happy about that and having you back in town with them."

Her gaze came back toward him. "Yeah, they're the best parents I've ever had."

Tate almost chuckled, but her serious expression held him back. "You got lots of hugs tonight from the townspeople.

I take it you've been gone awhile."

"Ten years." Brooke shoved off the railing, stepped down the steps, and walked away.

Tate followed, keeping in step with her slow pace. Why had Brooke been gone that long? From the hugs and happy squeals from the Crawdad Beach people, she was well-liked.

They walked along the quiet road. The porch lights cast a welcoming glow along the street. Tate breathed deep of the crisp, cool evening. The sound of a dog barking in the distance broke into the quiet.

"How did you get into welding?" Brooke asked as she glanced toward him.

"It wasn't what I thought I'd do. I always wanted to be an NFL wide receiver. But life took a different turn—a wicked hit during a game messed up my leg, which caused me to lose a four-year college scholarship." Tension built at the memory. Tate rubbed the back of his neck. "My parents are good, hardworking people but aren't wealthy. I didn't want them to take out a big loan for college, so I went to trade school. It turned out okay. I enjoy working with my hands, fixing and creating things."

"I like that, too." Brooke grinned as her gaze caught in his.

He could appreciate a woman who liked hard work. Throughout the evening, he'd noticed how she hadn't stopped packing, cleaning, and moving boxes until everything was ready for Jeremy and Grace. Tate's attention dropped to Brooke's lips, and he quickly focused on the road ahead. "Did you play sports?"

"No way," Brooke said with a soft laugh. "I have absolutely no coordination, and I used to be kind of pudgy."

"I find that hard to believe. Tate glanced over at her, appreciating the view. "You're in great shape." She was a knockout.

Brooke's gaze flitted to his, then quickly turned away. "You're kind to say so."

"I'm not just saying that. You're a beautiful woman." If she didn't realize that, she needed to know. Too many people were quick to criticize and find fault; not enough were encouragers. He knew that fact first-hand.

"Thank you." She didn't look at him.

Since she was obviously uncomfortable, he rerouted the conversation. "What brought you back to Crawdad Beach?"

Brooke was quiet for so long that Tate wasn't sure she heard him.

"I'm not sure," Brooke finally said. "No, that's not true. I think God brought me back." She gazed his way. "Does that sound strange?"

Tate shook his head. "Not in the least. My dad used to quote the verse that says a man plans his way, but the Lord directs his steps."

Brooke stopped, her gaze searching his. "Do you think God does that even when we aren't following him?"

"I do." He tried to choose his words carefully. "Think about all the people in the Bible who messed up or had bad things happen to them. God helped and got them rerouted to where they needed to go and who they needed to be." Tate paused. "God did that for me."

Brooke tilted her head, studying him. She took a few steps and stopped. "You're a good guy, Tate."

He stood a little taller, then dropped his shoulders. "No, I'm not that good." His many regrets still haunted him.

"I think you are." She took a step closer and kissed him on the cheek. "Thank you."

Brooke gulped as she stared at Tate's wide eyes. Why had she kissed him? At least it was on his cheek and not on his mouth. And, of course, that's right where she looked next. "I'm sorry."

Tate chuckled. "For what?"

"I shouldn't have done that. I barely know you."

"You don't have anything to be ashamed about. We haven't known one another long, but I already consider you a friend."

"You do?" Brooke hated that she sounded so needy. "I'm sorry about talking about God too. I used to get so tired of Maybelline always having a Bible story or a verse to share whenever I talked to her, and now I'm wanting that and doing the same thing." She was becoming like Maybelline, her true mom. At that thought, Brooke puffed out a laugh. Was this part of God remaking her? She giggled and thumped Tate on the chest. "Oh, my goodness. Tate, it's happening."

He stood there staring at her, probably thinking she'd lost her mind. Maybe she had. She giggled again.

Tate dipped his head to look at her more closely. "Are you okay?"

"Yes! I think God is working on me. He's remaking me. The new creation Brooke 2.0 is coming together." Brooke resumed the walk. "God does things just like that." She snapped her fingers. "Fascinating, don't you think?" She looked over her shoulder to make sure Tate was following.

He caught up with her. "It is fascinating." Even in the dim light, she could see a sparkle in his eyes.

"Did you have moments like this?"

Tate's eyebrows raised. "Like this?"

"I mean God moments where it's kind of like God peels back the darkness and lets you see the light." Brooke stepped up on the front porch of her parent's house. Oh my goodness, she did it again! She thought of the Taylors house as her parent's home. All of a sudden, it all clicked together: Chester and Maybelline were her parents, and she was supposed to be in Crawdad Beach. She really was home.

Brooke grabbed Tate's arm. "What is the verse that says something about such a time as this."

He blinked as though trying to process. "Give me a minute. It's from the book of Esther where Esther's uncle reminded her that she was put there for such a time as this to save their people."

"Right. That's it. So, God put me, *us*," Brooke waved her hand between them, "here for such a time as this. Is that cool, or what?"

Tate grinned. "It is cool."

Taking a deep breath, Brooke sighed. "Thanks for walking me home."

"You're more than welcome." Tate did a slight bow. "It's been my pleasure."

She unlocked the door, stepped inside, and turned toward him. "Thanks again."

He leaned closer, and his gaze dropped to her lips and then back to her eyes. "Thank you. I'll see you tomorrow."

She watched him walk away, amazed she'd found a good friend.

Chapter 16

"**M**om, Dad, I'm home!" Brooke called as she ran into the family room.

Chester almost fell off the couch as he hurried to stand. "You called me dad?" His teary-eyed gaze held a look of awe as he gazed at her.

"Yep, I did. I'm sorry I didn't say it sooner."

He put his arms around her, pulled her into a fatherly embrace, and kissed the top of her head. "Thank you. Brooke. Those are the sweetest words ever."

Maybelline squirmed in to join the embrace. "Welcome home, sweet girl."

"I finally realized I *am* home," Brooke squeezed them tight. "You're my parents. I'm so lucky. I mean, I'm so blessed."

"We are the blessed ones," Maybelline said.

Brooke stood safe in their arms. Why hadn't she realized the truth sooner? Not just about her parents, but about God? She felt like her heart had found a home, not just with her parents but with Him. She gave them both a big squeeze and stepped back. "Now that I know I belong here, I want to look into buying that house."

Maybelline and Chester smiled at one another, then

Brooke. Maybelline took Brooke's hand in hers. "We have some news about Mrs. Chapman's house."

Brooke's lip trembled. Just when she was thinking, things were falling into place.

"It's good news," Chester said with a big grin.

"Okay." Brooke drew out the word. "Is it still for sale?"

"Yes," Maybelline nodded. "I called and talked to Mrs. Chapman's daughter again, and she wants to go ahead and sell as soon as possible. So, she lowered her price."

Brooke sucked in a breath. "She did? Can I afford it?"

"Don't you want to go look at it first?" Chester asked as he held up a key and waved it toward her. "The daughter left this with a neighbor who is a good friend. We can look at it in the morning and make sure it's something you want to buy."

"Yes, I'd love to. But what if I can't afford it?"

"You have enough, Brooke," Maybelline said. "The house will need some work, so the price is for it to be sold as is." Maybelline paused. "She only wants seventy-five thousand for the house."

"Really? That nice house for that price? Oh, my goodness. I can buy that. I really can. I have enough for a down payment and could get a loan for what was left." Brooke did a little happy dance.

She cracked up when Maybelline and Chester joined in. Not any of them were coordinated, but it sure was fun.

Tate stepped out on his back screened-in-porch and stared at the house behind him where Brooke lived. He rubbed his beard where she'd kissed him and said he was a good guy.

But she didn't know him and sure didn't know the mistakes he'd made.

Sure, he wanted to be a good guy and be a hero. He used to watch the old westerns and swashbuckling movies with his grandpop. Tate wanted to be the guy who rode in on a white horse or sword-fought to rescue a damsel in distress. Then he wanted to be the best hero football player.

But none of those things happened. He'd miserably failed.

Tate kicked a patio chair and went inside.

Brooke walked next to her parents as they approached the house. She barely got a moment's sleep last night because she was so excited. Grinning and teary-eyed, she thought about having a mom and dad who loved her and that she might be able to have her own home, which would be only two doors down from Grace and two blocks away from her parents.

"The house was built in 1918 and is one of Crawdad Beach's historic homes." Chester handed Brooke the key as they stepped onto the front porch.

"It was a beauty when we first moved to town,"

Maybelline added. "Mrs. Chapman was known as a woman of faith and passionate about prayer. I was blessed to attend the Bible study she had in her home."

Brooke unlocked the door and stepped inside. Chester and Maybelline followed. No one said anything, as though they'd entered a sacred, peaceful place.

Tall ceilings about twelve feet tall and wainscotting about Chester's height lined the foyer walls. The hardwood floors were worn but looked in excellent condition. To the right was a large opening leading into a living room with a vintage-looking fireplace.

"This is where we used to have Bible study," Maybelline said in a hushed voice.

Brooke could almost picture a group of older ladies gathered together to study the Bible. No wonder the house felt so peaceful. She turned to the left, where another opening with pocket doors led to a room that could be used as a study or dining room.

While her parents followed, Brooke walked down the hall and peeked inside a bathroom with white subway tile, a clawfoot tub with a vintage-looking shower attachment, a toilet, a pedestal sink, and a medicine cabinet that looked like she'd stepped back in time.

Beyond that was another bedroom and a larger one with a small, more modern bathroom with a shower, toilet, and sink.

Excited to see the rest, Brooke hurried to the kitchen: the cabinets and appliances were older but well-kept, and an original farmhouse sink sat under a window overlooking the backyard. A tiny back porch was off the kitchen. Most of the house looked original, as if it had been cocooned in time.

"You probably need to have a home inspection before you buy," Chester advised. "I can call Katherine Mitchell to have a look. She's the builder who renovated most of the buildings and many houses in the area."

Brooke nodded. "That would be good, but even if she finds something wrong, I would love to buy this house." She felt like the home was hugging her, as if this was where she belonged.

"I can understand why you feel that way," Maybelline said as she looked around. "It has a warmth to it. Mrs. Chapman was raised in this house, and she loved her home. I can't imagine how many thousands of prayers were prayed while she lived here. Her daughter loves the house, too, but she lives in Texas, and that's her home now. But, she wants to sell the home to someone who will take care of it like Mrs. Chapman did."

Maybelline's arm came around Brooke's shoulder. "If you want the house, we will gladly help you in any way you need."

"Thank you. I do want it."

"Our baby girl is getting her first house." Chester sniffled. "Let's call Mrs. Chapman's daughter and get the ball rolling."

Feeling ridiculously teary-eyed, Brooke turned away and tried to compose herself. Never in a million years did she think she'd be able to have a home this nice. Casting a quick glance upward, Brooke whispered a prayer of thanks.

Chapter 17

"He's absolutely perfect," Brooke said as she cradled Jeremy's and Grace's baby. "Hello, William Johnson." Brooke kissed the sleeping baby's downy-soft head.

Beaming a big smile, Grace sat next to them on the couch. "Thank you for all you and Tate and the rest of the town did to get the house ready for us."

"It was our pleasure. I hope we arranged everything okay."

"It looks great. And it was so nice to step into our home and not worry about setting everything up. Plus, having William's room ready was a huge help."

The baby squirmed and looked like he was getting ready to fuss. "I think he's wanting his momma." Brooke carefully handed William back.

Grace grinned as she nestled her baby in her arms. "That's such a strange and wonderful thing to think about. I'm actually a mom."

A twinge of envy rolled through Brooke's chest. Would she ever have the opportunity to be a mother? If she did, hopefully, God would help her to be much better than her birth mother. "You and Jeremy will be great parents."

"I hope so. I'm sure we'll make mistakes, but I want

William always to know he's loved." Grace stroked her son's sweet head.

"It's a shame that's not true for every child." What would her life have been like if her parents had loved her when she was little? Brooke got to her feet. She couldn't change her first fourteen years, and wishing and whining about the past never helped. She had parents who loved her now, and she would not get trapped again in the Grrrs.

"I wish I could go back and rewrite your story." Grace took Brooke's hand.

"Thanks. That would be nice. I know you have many years you'd also like to rewrite." Brooke squeezed her friend's fingers, then crossed to the door. "The past can't be changed, but God is showing me how to move forward. I better get to work before I get in trouble."

"No rush." Grace grinned. "I know the owners, and they're pretty lenient people. Before you go, I'm so excited you're going to buy Mrs. Chapman's house."

"Me too. I can't wait." At least owning a home was one dream that could come true.

"One more thing. Jeremy and I want to gift you some furniture from the store."

"Aww, thank you. That's so sweet of you. Chester and Maybelline, I mean Mom and Dad, are buying me a couch and chairs."

"You might have had a rough start in life, but at least things are working out now."

"Looks that way, doesn't it?" Brooke smiled at the

thought. "I'll see you later."

She arrived at the workshop and checked her to-do list. So far, she'd completed five large, fourteen medium, and twenty-six small projects. Jeremy and Grace loved what she'd done, and evidently, their customers did too since most of the furniture had already sold.

Brooke walked around the shop, looking at all the possibilities of what could be repurposed or created. The old would be made new—kind of like her life. She had parents who loved her, she'd be a homeowner soon, and she had a job she enjoyed. What else could she want?

One very handsome person came to mind.

A sound behind Brooke drew her attention, and she turned to find Tate walking toward her. She grinned. Maybe she should think about him more often.

Tate smiled. "I called out when I stepped into the building, but you must not have heard me. You looked deep in thought."

Looking at his handsome face, heat radiated to Brooke's cheeks. She shoved her hands in her back pockets. She was actually blushing? Who did that kind of thing? She wasn't a blusher. Her hot cheeks said otherwise. "Hi, I was just thinking about what projects to do next." *Among other things.*

"Then I have perfect timing." Tate stopped beside her. "Could I borrow you for a few minutes?"

"Of course."

"I printed off possible project ideas I could make to sell at Knick Knacks." Tate motioned toward one of the work tables, took papers out of his back pocket, and spread them out in front of them. "Which ones do you think would be best?"

Brooke stood next to Tate, their shoulders touching. She could tell he'd been working but still smelled clean like he'd just had a shower. She tried not to lean in closer. "These are all great ideas. Grace said many of their customers are staying at the beach and drive over to shop, so maybe a few smaller items that would be easier for those who are traveling would be best."

"Sounds good," Tate said. "So, if you were a customer, which ones would you like best?"

Enjoying being close to him, she took her time surveying his papers. "I really like the laser-cut clock designs and wall art." She looked his way. "You can make things like this?"

"Yep. I can program the machine for anything from industrial projects to simple designs."

Ideas ran through her mind on some fun projects, plus it would be a nice way to spend additional time with Tate. "Maybe we could work together on a few things."

"That'd be great." Tate grinned. "If you're free this evening, we could have a brainstorming session."

"Brainstorm, huh?" She leaned against the workbench and raised an eyebrow. "Sounds like a challenge."

Seeing Brooke get a little sassy, Tate stood taller and

puffed out his chest. "I am up for *any* challenge. Six o'clock, my place. My brain will be in gear, and I'll even have pizza ready when you arrive."

"Dinner and brainwork?" Brooke grinned. "I'll be there."

"Good." Tate gave her his own sassy-type grin as he gathered up his papers. "Bring your brain, and we'll see what we can come up with."

"See you soon," Brooke said with a way-too-kissable smile.

Tate moved his focus to his watch. Without looking again in her direction, he hurried back to his building. He needed to finish his work for the day, run by the store to pick up supplies, shower, ensure his place was clean, and cook a pizza.

He would then spend the evening finding new ideas for his business and getting to know the beautiful Brooke Taylor better.

Chapter 18

"You sure do smell nice. Look nice, too."

Brooke grinned at her dad's comments as she walked toward the patio door. She wasn't dressed up, but her jeans and shirt were clean and new. "Tate and I are just going to discuss ideas for his business."

"Do you need to take anything to eat?" Her mom asked from the kitchen.

"No, ma'am. He's making pizza."

"Have fun," Chester said with a sly grin.

"Oh, I will." Brooke wiggled her eyebrows. She giggled as her dad's sudden expression changed to a more worried look. "I'll be good."

He gave a nervous chuckle. "I know you will."

"See you both later." Brooke hurried out the door before thinking of more ways to tease her parents. It felt good to enjoy being with them without worrying. She crossed through the backyard, came around the front to Tate's side of the duplex, and knocked.

Tate greeted her with a smile as he opened the door and stepped aside to let her enter. "Thanks for coming over."

She entered an open living area with light blue walls and plank wood vinyl flooring. The furniture consisted of a soft white couch, two brightly colored floral chairs, a coffee table, and a flat-screen television perched on a white cabinet. The rear of the room contained the kitchen and dining area. "Nice place," Brooke said.

"Yeah, it's good. It came furnished. I wouldn't have chosen foo-foo chairs." Tate wrinkled his nose.

She chuckled at his description of the floral chairs. "Foo-foo?"

"That's more my style." He pointed to the television of a video showing the inside of a beautiful log cabin in the mountains with a roaring, crackling fire in the stone fireplace. "I thought this would work for a little ambiance."

Brooke hummed in agreement. "I'd love a place like that."

Tate shot an appreciative look her way. "You like the mountains?"

"I do. I was able to go several times when I was younger." One of her foster families had a small cabin in the Smokies. During the summer, she and the other kids would play in the river and climb the hills, and at night, they would sit around a firepit toasting marshmallows. Why had she forgotten good memories like that? Fenton used to say that too many people miss the good things in their lives because they stay focused on bad things. Brooke sighed. She'd done that for too many years.

Tate stood beside her, gazing at the video. "The mountains have a soothing effect on them. I worked in the Gatlinburg area for a few years where lots of craftsmen peddle their wares. I thought about settling down in that area, but for some reason, here I am." His gaze lingered on his face for a moment, and he smiled.

Brooke's heart skipped. Like a little kid? She tried not to roll her eyes at the idiot thought of a heart skipping. She wasn't a romantic type and had kept her distance from men for years. Why was she attracted to Tate? Just because he was nicely built, handsome, had kind blue eyes, and was a nice guy didn't mean she'd noticed. Much.

His gaze flicked to her lips and back to her eyes. Tate cleared his throat and backed away. "The pizza should be ready in a few minutes." He motioned toward his kitchen. "I also have a salad if you like healthy stuff."

"Both sound very nice. Thank you." She followed and leaned against the counter as she watched him work. "Can I help?"

Tate took the pizza out of the oven, laid it on his stovetop, and used the pizza cutter to make slices. "Sure. Would you get the salad and dressing out of the refrigerator?"

Brooke placed the salad and dressing on the already set table.

"I hope this is a good one." He moved the pizza over and placed it on a trivet. "The guy at the store said it was their best-selling." Tate held out a chair for her.

As she sat, she grinned up at him. "Thank you."

He nodded. "My mom wanted me to be a gentleman." His comment sounded more regretful than a statement. "Do you mind if I bless the food?"

"I will take any blessing you want to give."

"I can agree with that." Tate bowed his head and said a short but very sweet prayer. When he finished, he grinned. "Let's eat."

During the meal, Tate shared stories about some of the crazy antics he and Jeremy did as kids. "What about you? Were you up to mischief when you were younger?"

Brooke stared at her plate. What was she supposed to say? Most people didn't want to hear the negative things that happened in her life. During her foster years, she'd tried to stay in the background and avoid being seen, which didn't work enough of the time. She lifted her eyes to find Tate still waiting. "Not much to tell that's noteworthy." Why couldn't she come up with some witty, cute answer? Her brain seemed to have gone on hold as soon as she'd stepped into his duplex.

They continued eating quietly. Why couldn't she be a riveting conversationalist? Or be sexy, stare at his blue eyes, and flip her hair over her shoulder as she gave Tate a coy look? Nope. She didn't know what to say, and she sure didn't know how to be sexy or coy, plus her hair was short.

Brooke sighed. She didn't even know how to do that eyelash flutter thing she read in romance novels. She was just plain and knew more about working with her hands than working on anything of a romantic nature.

Tate placed his napkin on the table. "If you're finished, we can discuss ideas."

"Sounds good." Brooke picked up her plate and helped him clear the table.

While they cleaned the kitchen, Tate kept the

conversation going with polite small talk. Brooke couldn't figure out what to say or how to act. She wasn't uncomfortable with Tate. She liked and was attracted to him, which made her thoughts and words vanish into thin air.

Brooke whimpered. She'd become an airhead.

With his beautiful new friend, Tate felt like a babbling idiot talking about anything and everything. He'd pay money to find out what Brooke was thinking. Then again, he might not appreciate knowing her thoughts since she looked a little skittish around him. Maybe she didn't like him and was just being neighborly by coming over tonight.

Tate rubbed his hand over his bearded chin. Maybe he'd spent too much time on the road instead of settling down and dating in a serious fashion. It wasn't like he hadn't dated before, but it had been several years.

This wasn't even a date, and he was nervous and discombobulated. Brooke was beautiful and smelled wonderful. He thought she was attracted to him, but now she wouldn't even look his way.

Tate grabbed his laptop off the kitchen counter and brought it to the table. "Let me show you my ideas." He opened the file with links to the projects he'd found online and clicked on the first ones.

Brooke moved her chair close to him and leaned toward the monitor.

As he scrolled through the ideas he'd found, she seemed more comfortable, and her excitement grew as they discussed projects they could work on together.

Brooke might not be romantically interested in him, but at least he had a work buddy who was one of the most beautiful and sexiest women he'd ever seen.

Chapter 19

After lunch today, she was set to close on her new house. Brooke grinned. She would have her very own home!

Since the first time she had dinner at Tate's house, he'd come over every day for the last three weeks to work with her on items to sell at Knick Knacks. She felt bad that he spent so much time with her when he could be making his own products, but she didn't feel bad enough to want him to stop.

She'd never known anyone like Tate. He was kind and fun to be with, and he made her feel comfortable. He had the cutest grin and was very handsome.

Brooke gave herself a mental head shake and tried to focus on her latest project of turning an old armoire into a coffee bar. She'd removed the doors and sanded off the old finish. Unfortunately, there was a deep scar on the right side of the armoire. Brooke stepped closer and surveyed the damage. She could use a wood filler.

"Hey," Tate said as he walked toward her. "What are you working on?"

She grinned at her friend. "I'm trying to figure out what to do about this gouge in the wood."

He ran his hand along the edge. "Don't do anything. Scars add character and bring beauty to the wood."

"You think so?" Brooke stared at Tate.

"Yeah." Tate nodded. "Scars and what some people see as imperfections tell a story. Some people might not like them, but I think it adds a nice touch."

She rubbed the scar on her arm. "Too bad it's different on people." Ugh. Why was she being so wimpy? Wasn't Brooke 2.0 supposed to be strong and brave, forget the past, and smile at the future? Obviously, she was miserably failing at the new creation thing the Bible talked about.

"I have a doozy on my leg," Tate said. "My scar used to make me angry because it marked how my dream about playing in the NFL died, but the accident rerouted me to do what I love." He grinned her way. "I wouldn't be here without it."

She *was* grateful Tate moved here. But still... "They can be awful reminders of painful times."

"True, but they show what we've been through. They're proof of survival during hardships. If we lived through our wounds, that means we're survivors." Tate made a bodybuilder pose.

Brooke tried to smile, but she just couldn't. "I might have survived, but I'd rather not have the memories that go with scars,"

Tate's expression gentled. He stepped closer and wrapped his arms around her. "I'm sorry for whatever you've been through."

Surprised at his affection, Brooke stiffened and then relaxed. Desiring his warmth, she laid her head on his shoulder.

Tate held her close for a long time, his strong and steady heartbeat giving her comfort.

"My Grandpop was wounded several times in Vietnam." Tate's chest reverberated with his gentle baritone voice. "He had bullet and knife wounds and was hit with shrapnel. He said scars can glow with the testimonies of God's faithfulness because no matter how deep our wounds, God's love runs deeper, and His love turns everything into beauty."

She blinked at the thought of God turning her scars into something beautiful. How could *anything* beautiful come from what she'd been through? Brooke wanted to push away and refuse to listen to what Tate was saying, but part of her longed for the comfort he was giving.

Tate kissed the top of her head as if she belonged with him. "Grandpop said the scars of Jesus prove our lives were worth His suffering to save our lives."

Brooke wanted to nod in agreement because she knew all that and was grateful Jesus had saved her, but dealing with her scar, the visual reminder of what she'd been through, was so blasted difficult. Every day, she saw it, and every day, the horrible memory returned.

She pushed away. "I should have filled the scar with wood filler so I wouldn't have to listen to a sermonette." Brooke grimaced that she'd said that out loud. She didn't mean it, not really. But sometimes, it was hard to see beyond the wounds.

"I'm sorry." Tate's gaze was apologetic. "I didn't mean to

get preachy. It's just something I think about a lot. I didn't mean to make you uncomfortable."

Brooke stared at the floor. She didn't mean to make *him* feel bad. Tate was trying to be nice. She wanted to return to his arms, but she'd ruined the moment. "It's okay." She forced up a nice smile. "I appreciate what you shared. I guess I still need time to process a few things."

Tate mentally kicked himself as Brooke walked away, picked up a piece of sandpaper, and sanded the top of an old dresser.

Why hadn't he just kept the subject on woodworking? They had talked about God before; he even saw her at church on Sunday. Instead of giving her a lecture, he should have asked questions and found out what she was trying to process.

He came beside her and tried to get her attention. "Do you want to talk about it?"

Brooke shook her head. "No."

"Can I help you with a project?"

"Not today." Brooke didn't look at him. "I close on my house at lunch, so I'm not sure when I'll be back."

He gave her a big grin. "That's great about the house. Congratulations."

She didn't respond; just continued sanding.

Tate shoved his hands into his back pockets. "I guess I'll see you tomorrow?"

"Sure. I'll see you later."

Feeling dismissed, Tate returned to his building. He should have handled the scar discussion better. It wasn't like it had been easy for him to process and get over his injury. Still, what made Brooke get so upset?

What if something terrible had happened to her? Tate dropped into his office chair and placed his head in his hands. He hated that anyone had scars, especially women. And the thought of Brooke dealing with something made his stomach turn.

He needed to be more careful with his words and actions. He'd screwed up before, and he couldn't stand to make another mistake.

He still prayed for the young woman he'd left in the hotel years ago and wondered what had caused her scar. He groaned. How he wished he could go back in time and do things differently.

Chapter 20

With her packet of papers showing she was a new homeowner in one hand and her house key in the other, Brooke smiled as she stood on the porch of her new home.

Maybelline nudged her. "Are you excited?"

"Yes, but I still can't believe it's true." Brooke shuddered in excitement.

"Well, step inside and enjoy your new home," Chester prodded.

Brooke opened the door and jerked back. "Who refinished the floors?"

"Well," Chester grinned. "We didn't want you to have to worry about that."

"And you painted the walls?" Brooke couldn't believe her eyes.

"Why do you think we kept asking you so many questions about how you planned to decorate when you moved in?" Maybelline said. "I hope we didn't go too far with trying to help. The house still needs plenty of work, but we wanted enough done so you could move in whenever you wanted."

Chester stepped closer. "We're not trying to get rid of you. We didn't want you to worry about as much."

A chuckle of air burst out of Brooke as she looked around. "This is too good to be true. I thought it would take me a month to refinish the floors and repaint the rooms." She looked at her parents. "How much do I owe you?"

Chester held up his hand. "You don't owe us anything. It was our pleasure to take care of our little girl. We brought all the boxes from your trailer and moved them into the spare bedroom. Katherine Miller donated a refrigerator and oven from a house she was restoring. So, when do you want your couch and chairs to be delivered?" Chester asked as he wandered around the living area. "And we can bring your bedroom suite in whenever you're ready."

Okay, that did it. Brooke's eyes swelled with tears. "Oh, my goodness. You are all too nice to me."

"Oh, sweet girl." Her mom wrapped her in a big hug. "We love you. Plus, we had the best time sneaking around to get this done before closing."

"Yep," Chester chuckled, "made us feel like kids again.

"We did have assistance," Maybelline said. "Jeremy and Grace helped with cleaning while I got to spoil the baby. Henry came over to help, and Tate refinished the floors and painted the parts that needed a ladder."

Brooke closed her open mouth. "Why would you all do that for me? How did Tate have time to help? For the last three weeks, he's been at the workshop with me or in his building."

Chester grinned. "He's been here working at the crack of dawn."

Now Brooke really wanted to cry. Her parents and friends had been sweet to her, and she'd been a wimpy, not-so-nice person to Tate the last time they were together. He spent what little free time he had to help get her house ready, and he'd been helping her with tons of projects for Knick Knacks.

Tate had to be the nicest guy she'd ever known. He cared about her. She knew she liked him, but his level of sweetness tipped him over into a brand new category beyond just liking him. She didn't just like him. She loved him.

Brooke's heart felt like it was jumping up and down, telling her to get moving. She had to tell him that she loved him. "Can we wait until this weekend?" Brooke moved toward the door. "And would you mind if I see you both later today? I need to take care of something."

Although both looked surprised, her parents nodded and walked out before her.

Brooke locked the door, then wrapped them both in a big hug. "I love you both so much. Thank you for being such great parents. I'll see you later." She left them standing on the porch as she ran to her car.

Five minutes later, Brooke parked and ran inside Tate's building. She had to thank him and tell her what she was thinking and feeling.

Wearing his welding helmet, Tate had his back to her as he welded what looked like iron railings.

Brooke paced back and forth as she waited.

Tate finally shut off his welding torch, stowed the wand,

and removed his helmet. He ran his hands through his hair and turned toward her. "Hey. What are you doing here?"

She ran to where he was standing and placed a big kiss on his wonderful lips. "I came to thank you."

He chuckled. "Whatever I did, you are more than welcome."

"I'm so sorry about earlier. I want to thank you for all your help in the workshop. And I found out you've been working on the house I just bought. That's so sweet. Why are you so nice to me? I'm not anything special."

Tate took her in his arms. "Brooke, you have no idea what a wonderful woman you are." He kissed her in such a soft, sweet, and gentle way that she felt as if she was floating. Did she even have legs anymore?

Brooke kissed him back, wanting him to know how much she cared. The kisses continued until she was sure her lips had swollen double their size.

She'd never told anyone she loved them before, but she wanted to say the words to Tate. But what if he didn't love her? Maybe she could say I love you in French. That way, she could tell him, but he wouldn't know what she was saying.

"Je t'aime," she whispered in his ear.

Tate drew back. He held her face in his hands, smoothing his thumbs across her cheeks. "Je t'aime, mon amour."

Brooke gulped. "You know French?"

"I took four years of French in high school."

"Oh." She gave a nervous laugh. "I wanted to tell you I loved you but was afraid to, so I said it in French."

"You don't have to be afraid. I love you, Brooke Taylor. Thank you for loving me."

Brooke felt like she was in a fairy tale. How could he love her? "Really?"

"Yes, really." Tate kissed her hand like she was a maiden in a fairy tale.

"Can we kiss again?"

He chuckled. "Anytime you want would be fine with me."

Brooke gave him another kiss and a few more. She loved Tate, and he loved her. She sighed.

But if she loved him and he loved her, he needed to know who she really was. She just hoped he wouldn't run away.

She squirmed out of the embrace and stepped away. "Have you read the Book of Ruth?"

Tate gave her a curious glance. "The Bible account? Yeah, sure."

"You know who Boaz's mom was, right?"

"Rahab, the hero from the book of Joshua who rescued the Israelite spies."

"Yes, but she was also Rahab, the prostitute." Brooke whimpered that she would have to say the rest. "My mom was a prostitute."

Tate's eyebrows rose to his hairline. "Maybelline was a prostitute?"

"No!" Brooke held up her hands. "No, not her. I'm adopted."

"Whew!" Tate gave a nervous chuckle. "You had me worried for a moment. I couldn't imagine Maybelline in that line of work."

"You aren't upset about my mom?"

"No," Tate said with a shrug. "Why would I be? That's not who you are."

Brooke's lip trembled as she thought about that night years ago when she'd made a terrible mistake. "But, I haven't always been good."

"I've made mistakes, too." His gaze kept a tight hold on her as he stepped closer, close enough to wipe the tear trailing down her cheek. "I'm not proud of everything I've done. I love you. It doesn't matter who your mother was or what you've done. Je t'aime, Brooke Taylor."

Tate sealed his statement with sweet kisses as her heart breathed a relieved, happy sigh.

Chapter 21

"They called me Tater Tot."

Brooke stared at Tate as he helped her carry a big dresser in the workshop so she could get it refinished. "No way. Why would they do that?"

"My full name is Tate Oliver Tillman, and thus, the initials of TOT. I was overweight as a kid, so my classmates called me Tater Tot. When I finally had a growth spurt, I thinned out enough to go from being a puffy lineman to a svelte and swift running back." He set down the dresser and curled his arm, showing a very impressive bicep.

"You turned out very nice, Mr. Tillman." Brooke giggled as she moved toward him.

"And you are one mighty fine-looking woman." He pulled her into his arms and kissed her.

"I love you, Tate." Enveloped in Tate's hug, Brooke cradled her cheek on his shoulder.

"I love you, too. It's nice to say that, isn't it?"

"It's wonderful."

"Yes, it is. So, what are your initials?"

"Since I'm Brooke Ann Taylor. I guess I'm a BAT."

Tate chuckled as he kissed her. "You're the cutest bat I have ever seen."

"Alright, you two, get back to work." Chester chuckled as he walked toward them. "I realize you've been dating for three months, so it's amazing that anything is getting done around here."

With a playful expression, Tate released Brooke and raised an eyebrow. "I'll have you know, Mr. Taylor, that we have accomplished more in the last few months than we did before we officially started dating."

Chester chuckled. "I know that. Just had to give you a hard time. Thanks for treating our little girl so well."

"It's an honor." Tate swung his gaze toward Brooke. "She's special."

"Yes, she is." Chester smiled and gave her a gentle pat. "I came by to see if you needed any help today. Maybelline has some women meeting for a book club in our family room. They had read one of those Christian romantic fiction books together. Maybelline thought it was best I wasn't there to spoil the fun."

"You don't like romance?" Tate grinned.

"Pfft." Chester waved his hand as though he didn't care. "Romance. Who needs to read about stuff like that."

Brooke laughed. "You are the most romantic man I've ever known. I bet you read the book, didn't you?'

Chester threw her a mock glare. "I will neither confirm nor deny that possibility."

"I love it! My dad reads romance." Brooke chuckled.

"Well, it was a good one," he muttered. "Everyone needs a happy ending." Chester smiled at her, then turned a semi-serious gaze to Tate.

"I agree." Tate nodded.

"Good," Chester said. "So, how can I help today?"

Brooke glanced around the workshop. "Would you be willing to take apart and remove the nails of the old pallets stacked over there?"

Chester looked to where she'd pointed. "You bet. Don't let me disturb you two lovebirds. Just pretend I'm not here."

Brooke giggled. "Yeah, right."

"I probably need to get back to my building. I'll see you tonight at your place for dinner. Call me if you need anything."

"I always need you." Brooke smiled at her handsome boyfriend.

Tate grabbed her and gave her a big kiss. He stepped back with a satisfied look, then glanced toward Chester. "I kissed your daughter and love her, Mr. Taylor." With a laugh, Tate ran out the door.

"Young affectionate whippersnapper, kissing my sweet girl," Chester mumbled. He grinned at Brooke. "Good thing I like him."

"Thanks, Dad. I like him, too."

Tate let his thoughts wander as he focused on his laser machine. How did he get so lucky? He was seriously dating a gorgeous woman. The more time they spent together, the more relaxed Brooke was around him, and the more her cute personality came out.

Was it too early in their relationship to make long-range plans? He didn't want to wait since they were both trying to be good, which was getting more complex every time they were together.

Maybe he needed to read a Christian romance novel to get ideas on loving someone without taking them to bed. He chuckled, thinking about Chester reading a book like that. Tate grimaced as he considered what Brooke's dad would do to him if he misused his precious daughter.

The machine finished cutting the material for his latest projects, and Tate moved the pieces to his work table. He needed, no wanted, to go ahead and ask Brooke to marry him. He had enough regrets in his past, and he didn't need to hesitate this time to do what he felt was the right thing.

Chapter 22

Rolls were warming in the oven, the rice was cooked and ready, and the salad was already on the table. Brooke rechecked the Shrimp Creole, ensuring it tasted good. With a yum, she closed the lid. She might not be a master chef, but it was pretty good for her first try using Maybelline's secret recipe.

Brooke loved what Tate and others had done to help her remodel her kitchen. Cabinets had been painted and new hardware added, the old ceramic tile counters replaced with wood countertops, white beadboard was used as a backsplash, she'd repurposed an antique dresser to be her kitchen island, and had refinished a bistro table to use in her breakfast nook.

Her phone signaled that someone had stepped on her porch, and she could see Tate through the front doorbell camera. Even though Crawdad Beach was a safe place to live, her parents had insisted she install a security system. They'd even purchased it for her.

Tate leaned close to the camera and made a goofy grin.

She chuckled as she ran to let him inside. "Hi, handsome. Want a kiss?"

"Hey, beautiful." He cupped her face in his hands and

granted her request. "I didn't think you'd be serving dessert first."

"Life's too short not to enjoy every moment." Brooke grinned as she motioned for him to follow her to the kitchen. "I hope you like Shrimp Creole."

"I love it." Tate stood beside her as she spooned the rice and creole into serving dishes.

"Is there anything you don't like?" He was too easy to please.

He glanced up at the ceiling before returning his gaze to her. "I'm not a fan of liver and onions." He shuddered. "Besides that, I'm open to trying anything."

"I had liver once," Brooke wrinkled her nose, "and once was way too much."

"Good, then I don't ever have to worry about coming home to a plate of the stuff."

Brooke's eyebrows hiked as she stared at him. *Coming home?*

He cleared his throat, picked up the dishes, and placed them on the table.

Tate mentally kicked himself. He hadn't meant to say that out loud. Just because he was thinking about marriage didn't mean it was the right time. He still didn't have a ring and wasn't sure if he needed to ask Chester's permission.

Was that even still a thing? Did guys still do stuff like that?

He'd need to check the internet tonight for the latest information.

Giving Tate a curious glance, Brooke set a basket of fresh rolls on the table. "Have a seat. We don't want it to get cold."

"Right." He held out her chair, waited until she was seated, and sat across from her. "Thanks for making dinner. It smells wonderful."

"You're welcome."

Since she was grinning and staring at him, he bowed his head and said a quick prayer.

As they ate, he kept complimenting her on the meal and talking about what he was working on and the projects he hoped they could do together. He knew he was rambling, but he couldn't seem to stop talking. Of course, he did not speak with his mouth full. But he did chew faster than usual.

After the meal, he helped her clean the kitchen, and they moved to her living area.

An open cardboard box sat on her coffee table. Tate peeked inside.

Brooke sat on the couch and curled her legs under her. "Those are old photos that my mom brought over."

He picked up a picture of a girl with long hair. "Is this you?" Something about her looked familiar.

"Yes. I was pretty chubby when I was younger. I didn't have my growth spurt until my freshman year in college."

"You had long hair?" A sudden queasiness swirled in his stomach as Tate stared at the photo. Surely, he was mistaken.

"Yeah, until about ten years ago." Brooke's gaze shifted

away from him. Why was she uncomfortable?

Tate put the photo back in the box. "You were cute then, but now you're a beautiful woman."

A question in her eyes, Brooke's gaze came back to him. "You really think so?"

"Definitely! You're gorgeous, smart, fun to be with, talented, a great cook, an amazing craftsperson, and a wonderful kisser." He wiggled his eyebrows.

"You're wonderful, too." She stood and hugged him. "I love you, Tate."

"I love you, too." He placed his hand behind her neck, gently pulled her toward him, and pressed his lips to hers. He didn't understand what she saw in him, but he hoped and prayed one day she would be his wife.

She pulled back and grinned as she fanned her face. "Is it hot in here?" Brooke took off her long-sleeve shirt to reveal a cute t-shirt.

"Spring has arrived." Tate chuckled.

"I think it's more my hot boyfriend." She giggled as she rested her arms on his shoulders.

Shock gripped Tate's chest as he stared at the scar along Brooke's interior forearm. Was she the young woman he'd left at the hotel? No, surely not.

Brooke's smile faded. She grabbed her long-sleeve shirt, put it on, and walked away.

Tate groaned. What had he done?

Chapter 23

Brooke slammed the bathroom door and stared into the mirror. From the stunned expression on Tate's face, he obviously thought her scar was ugly. It *was* ugly and proof she'd gone through something horrible. She stifled a scream.

Tate was the one who lectured her about how scars could become beautiful with God's touch. He must think his scars were okay but not hers. She thought better of Tate, thought he would be the one who would love her. And now?

Brooke rammed her fists into her eyes, trying to stop the tears, but it was useless. A sob broke through and she cried for the things she'd been through and cried that she wouldn't have a future with Tate.

No man would ever love her.

A knock on the door made Brooke jump. "Go away!"

"No. I won't. We need to talk." Tate's voice broke. "I'm sorry, Brooke."

Was he apologizing because of his reaction to her scar? He better have a good explanation. She opened the door and glared at him.

Tate took her hands in his. "I've got to tell you something. It might be an answer to my prayers, or I'm not sure..."

"What are you talking about?" Brooke jerked back and

crossed her arms.

"I'm sorry about your scar. It's not that. It's something else." Tate blew out a breath as he gazed at the ceiling, then returned his eyes to her. "It's about something that happened about ten years ago."

A horrifying memory ran through Brooke's mind. She pushed past him and ran to her living area. Taking deep breaths, she tried to steady herself.

He came toward her. "It's about something that happened in a hotel."

Oh, God. Not that. She slammed her fists into his chest. "What are you talking about?"

"Please let me explain."

She shook her head as she fought off the memories. How would Tate know?

"Brooke. It's okay. Please let me tell you what happened. I didn't know it was you."

Oh, God, no! A sob broke out, and she crumpled to the hardwood floor. *Not him. Please, not him.*

He knelt beside Brooke and wrapped his arms around her. "Please don't cry. I love you. It's not what you think. Please let me tell you what happened."

Tate held Brooke as she sobbed. "Baby, it's okay. You were drunk, and those guys wouldn't leave you alone. I should have acted sooner to protect you."

Brooke's shocked, wide-eyed gaze met his. "*You* were at the sports bar?"

"Yes. I could tell you were upset and had been crying. I should have stepped in sooner."

She shoved him away and stumbled to her feet. "I had been crying because I *finally* tracked down my birth father and found out he was the scum of the earth." Brooke drew in a breath. "After that, I had driven for hours when I stopped to use the bathroom. And then those obnoxious guys wouldn't leave me alone and gave me something to drink, but it must have been drugged."

Brooke's eyes narrowed to slits as she punched Tate's chest. "You weren't one of them, were you?"

"No! I tried to help you."

She ran her hands through her hair, her eyes squinted in concentration. "I tried to get away from one guy, but I couldn't even see straight. He was pulling me outside." She shot her attention back to Tate. "Were you the man who hit the jerk that wouldn't leave me alone?"

"Yes." At least he'd tried to be a hero.

Brooke studied him warily. "But that man didn't have a beard."

"I was clean-shaven back then. Brooke, when the guy got back to his feet and came at you again, you," Tate paused, trying to put it in nicer terminology. "You expressed your displeasure."

Her nose wrinkled. "I threw up all over him."

"Yeah, that took care of him, but you still were in bad

shape. So, I took you to my hotel room where you'd be safe."

Brooke stared at him, her face going from beat red to pale. "I was so smashed I couldn't walk, and you took me to a *hotel*?"

Tate grimaced and prayed she would understand. "You had mumbled something about not living near there, and I didn't know where you lived or what car you drove. I wasn't going to leave you alone. You couldn't have driven, and I didn't know if those guys would come back again."

Fire lit Brooke's eyes. "So you took advantage of a woman who had either been given a drug or some strong alcohol and took me to your hotel room and put me in your bed!" Brooke hit him again.

"No! It's not like that." Tate rubbed his chest where she kept hitting him. "You could barely walk. I was going to let you have my room, and then I was going to sleep in my car. But when we got inside, you said you were going to be sick again, so I sat with you in the bathroom while you threw up."

She shook her head as though trying to remember. Her gaze swung back to him. "You held my hair for me so it wouldn't get in the way."

"Yes," He nodded. "But you still got it all over your shirt, so you took it off and passed out again. I tried not to look. So, I put you in the bed, washed your shirt in the sink, and hung it to dry in the bathroom. And then I slept on the floor next to you to make sure you would be okay. Brooke, nothing happened. I didn't do anything inappropriate, and neither did you."

Brooke's lip trembled as she puffed out a cry. "So, why did you leave me alone and throw a hundred-dollar bill on the floor?"

Tate groaned. "I didn't throw it on the floor. I had to get to my job and couldn't wake you. I kept trying. I was planning on leaving you a note, but I couldn't find anything to write on or write with. I had pulled out my wallet to see if I had something, and when I did, the bill must have fallen out."

He reached out to her, but she stepped away. "I didn't mean to leave money. I hoped and prayed you'd be okay until I got back to the room on my lunch break. But you were gone. And that's when I found out my money was missing."

Brooke stared at him, then gasped in a sob. "You didn't think I was a prostitute?"

"No! *Never* for a moment."

She sucked in another cry. "I thought I had turned out like my mother."

Tate drew her to his chest and held her tight as she cried. "Oh, Brooke. No, you didn't do anything wrong. I'm so sorry you thought I had left money like that. I *never* thought you were anything but a sweet girl caught in a bad situation. I was trying to help. I didn't ever mean to make you feel that way. You're wonderful, and I love you. Marry me, Brooke Taylor." He kissed the top of her head. "Please marry me."

Chapter 24

Tate hadn't meant to blurt out a proposal. It just happened. He wanted Brooke to marry him, but he hoped to do something much more romantic.

Brooke wiped her eyes and stared at him like he was a three-headed monster.

That wasn't the response he was hoping for. "Sorry about the timing. I do want to marry you." Since she was still staring at him, he gave a nervous chuckle. "Maybe I should just back away and do this another time."

She grabbed his shirt and pulled him toward her. "Are you serious?"

"About leaving or the proposal?"

"You want to marry me?" Brooke tilted her head and blinked several times.

"Yes, I do." Tate nodded. "Of course. I love you and want to be with you."

"But why?" Her bottom lip trembled.

Maybe he could at least attempt to be somewhat romantic. "How do I love thee? Let me count the ways. That's all I know about that poem or love letter, so let me give you my list. You're intelligent, an amazing craftswoman, fun to be with, gorgeous, a great kisser, and my heart hurts when I'm not with you."

Brooke raised an eyebrow. "Your heart probably hurts because I've been hitting you."

Tate rubbed his chest. "Yeah, there is that."

She moved away and plopped on the couch. "I love you and want to marry you, too. But I just found out that for *ten* years, I believed someone thought I was a prostitute. I quit school, ran away from my parents, and ran away from everything because of what happened that night." Hurt and anger mixed with her words as she wrung her hands.

"I'm sorry, Brooke." He slumped beside her. "I wish I could go back and change things."

"Ten long years," Brooke whispered. "Tate, I'm sorry. I need time to process." Her lips were in a tight frown, and she wouldn't even look at him

"I understand." He'd give her time but hoped this wouldn't end their relationship. Tate reached for her, and she dodged his touch.

He stood and put his hands in his back jeans pocket. "I'll see you later?"

When she didn't acknowledge his question, he felt like his heart had ripped out of his chest. He walked out the door and didn't look back.

Brooke shoved off the couch after Tate left. For ten stinking years, she worried and felt ashamed for something

that didn't even happen. She paced back and forth, thinking about how different her life could have been.

She spent most of her life worrying about the things her birth mother had done. Then she worried, thinking she'd done something like her mom. So many blasted wasted years!

Brooke checked the time. She needed to talk to someone. Maybe it wasn't too late. She sent a text to Grace to see if she could come over. Grace quickly replied that Jeremy was taking care of something at the shop, and the baby was asleep, so she could come on down.

A few minutes later, Brooke sat on the couch beside Grace and told her what really happened that night.

Her friend smiled and sighed in relief. "That's wonderful news. That's a completely different scenario than you had imagined. Sometimes, or most times, what we imagine is much worse than reality. Learning the truth is great news, isn't it?"

"Well, yeah, kinda." Brooke tugged a throw pillow into her lap. "But it messed up my life for ten stinking years."

"But you can start living now without worrying about that night."

"Easier said than done," Brooke mumbled.

A tiny sigh came from the baby monitor sitting on the coffee table. Grace leaned forward to listen before turning her attention back to Brooke. "I can understand why Tate might not have realized it was you, but why do you think you didn't recognize him?"

"Besides me being drugged or drunk, Tate didn't have a beard back then. Plus, I couldn't even see straight when he came to help me."

"I'm sorry about what happened, but at least Tate was trying to be a good guy. Jeremy thinks the world of his cousin. Tate's a nice man, Brooke."

"Yeah, I guess. I mean, I know he is. But, all those years, I thought he'd left money because I was a prostitute."

Grace tilted her head. "Isn't it a good thing that *wasn't* what happened and you now know the truth?"

"Yeah." Brooke shrugged. "But I've lost ten years, never finished college, and didn't talk to my parents. Not to mention, I've lived like a nun for a decade."

"You keep talking about losing ten years, but what if they aren't lost but part of the growing process and maybe even for your protection? It's easy to think things would have turned out better, but what if they had turned out much worse? What if you had stayed in college and got in with the wrong crowd or got involved with a bad guy? From what you shared about working in Fenton's shop, God kept you safe with him, his family, and his friends."

Brooke took a deep breath. She hadn't thought about that.

"So," Grace leaned closer, "are you going to let the past continue to ruin your future? You aren't responsible for what your mother did. You are your own woman, and you said Tate asked you to marry him. Brooke, you have a whole new life in front of you."

Grace laid her hand on Brooke's arm. "Tate's not the one who hurt you. The past can't be changed. Please stop allowing the things that happened and the what might have beens to destroy your future."

Brooke squeezed the pillow against her chest. Shouldn't she be ecstatic about learning the truth? No one thought she was a prostitute, and she hadn't done anything wrong that night. Tate was the one who rescued her and made sure she didn't fall into the hands of those obnoxious guys.

"Wasn't it the apostle Paul who said something about leaving the past behind and pressing on?" Grace's gentle voice continued. "I think it was in the book of Philippians. And in the Book of Isaiah, didn't God talk about doing new things?"

Brooke glanced at her friend and tried not to roll her eyes. "Yeah, I've heard those lines before. Maybelline's always quoting Bible verses."

"Maybe it's time to remember God loves you, the past is over, and you can leave the old behind and embrace the new that God has offered."

A light breeze rustled in the trees as Brooke sat on her porch steps. Stars hung in the night sky as though watching and waiting to see what she would do.

What if Tate hadn't been there that night? Brooke shuddered at the thought of what could have happened. But still, the question she needed to decide was whether she would keep allowing her past to mess up her future. She was so tired of replaying negative things in her head.

It was time to stop the guilt, remorse, regret, replaying the negative and shame, and get rid of the Grrrs! She was Brooke 2.0, not the old 1.0. God loved her and had made her a new creation. She'd been given new mercies and new opportunities. Plus, she had a man she loved and who loved her. It was time to leave the old and step into the new.

Brooke shoved off the porch and took off running.

Chapter 25

When Tate didn't answer his door, Brooke ran to the back and peeked inside his screened-in porch. He was sitting in the dark with his head resting in his hands.

Her throat tight, she quietly opened the screen door, which surprisingly didn't even make a creaking sound, tiptoed toward him, and laid her hand on his shoulder. "Tate?"

He looked up and rose to his feet. "Hey. Are you okay?"

"I am. I'm sorry about earlier. I have lots of junk in my past, and sometimes I don't deal well with it, but I'm trying to do better. And I love you, and I don't want to lose you. And if your offer still is available, I would love to marry you."

Tate smiled. "Of course, I want to marry you." He reached toward her.

"Wait," Brooke backed away. "Before we move forward, I need to tell you some things. Would you mind sitting back down for me, please?" She couldn't bear to watch his expression when she told him about her past.

"Okay." His gaze curious and wary, he sat in the chair and looked up at her.

She wrung her hands as she paced back and forth. "I was a foster kid. You know about my birth mother. The whole prostitute thing is bad enough. And I've had some decent foster families and others that were not good. Some people did bad things." Brooke rubbed the scar on her arm, then forced her hands back to her side. "And I've done things I'm not proud of, and I have nightmares, and sometimes something reminds me of my past, and it makes me sad or upset, and it might take me a little while to sort through that kind of stuff."

She nibbled on her lower lip as she stepped toward him. "So, if you're still willing to marry me, I would really, *really* like to marry you." Her voice broke as she prayed Tate would still want her.

He smiled as he rose to his feet and pulled her gently into his arms. "I am so sorry about all the pain in your past. Whatever you've been through, and whatever comes in the future, I will be here for you, and we'll trust that God will help us with it all. I can't change your past, but I would love to be part of your future." Tate caught her hands in his as he went down on one knee and looked up at her. "Brooke Taylor, will you please marry me?"

Brooke laughed in relief. "Yes, yes, yes!"

Her laughter was trapped by Tate's lips as he sealed their love with a volley of the sweetest kisses she'd ever known.

As much as he thoroughly enjoyed the moment, Tate stopped kissing Brooke. "I should ask your dad for permission. I want to start our life together on the right foot."

This time, he wanted to be the hero of her story.

"It's not like I'm a kid and need my dad's permission to do anything." Brooke glanced over her shoulder. "But their house lights are still on, and they don't usually go to bed until about 9:30." She grinned at him.

"Right." Tate hadn't planned on facing Chester right now, but getting it over with would be best. He took a deep breath and let it out as he steeled himself to face her father. "Okay. I'll do it."

Brooke took his hand in hers. "I'll be with you."

As much as he would love to have her next to him, Tate squeezed her fingers. "That'd be great, but I should do this alone. My back door is open if you want to go inside." Tate gave her another quick kiss before he lost his nerve. "I'll be back soon."

Praying for God's help, Tate crossed through their backyards and approached the front of their house. He stood on the porch momentarily, took another deep breath, sent up another prayer, and rang the doorbell.

Chester opened the door and gave him a curious look. "Hi, Tate, what's up?"

"Could I talk to you for a moment?"

"Sure." Chester stepped aside to let him enter. "Maybelline, we have a guest."

Maybelline rose from the couch and came toward him. "Hi, Tate. Everything okay?"

"Yes, ma'am. I was wondering if you wouldn't mind if I talked with Chester for a moment?"

She tilted her head and smiled. "Certainly. I'll be in the kitchen."

Tate glanced around the room containing the usual couch, chairs, and coffee table. Built-in bookshelves displayed family photos and numerous military awards for Chester. He was a military man? He was still in good shape and did have a posture that fit. Tate stood straighter.

Chester motioned toward the couch. "What's on your mind?"

Tate sat a cushion away. "I have something to ask you."

One of Chester's eyebrows rose. "What would you like to ask me?"

"I love your daughter. Brooke. And, I would like to ask your permission to marry her."

"You would, would you?"

"Yes, sir."

Chester looked up at the ceiling before turning a serious gaze toward Tate. "I do believe you love my daughter. However, are you prepared to love her, be faithful to her, and care for her even during life's difficulties as long as you live?"

"Yes, sir." Tate gave a firm nod. "I know it won't always be easy, and Brooke has told me some of the things she's been through. I realize she will need tender care, and with God's help, I believe we will have a good life together."

"Good answer." Chester didn't say anything else. He stared at Tate until perspiration ran down his back.

He tried not to squirm. Was he supposed to say something else?

Chester's eyes squinted as he leaned toward Tate. "You've already asked Brooke to marry you, haven't you?"

"Yes, sir." Tate tried not to lean back. "I'm sorry. It just happened. I should have done things the right way."

"She said yes?"

"Yes, sir."

"Well, that does it, then." Chester rose, grabbed Tate's hand, and pulled him to his feet. "Welcome to the family, son." Grinning, he shook Tate's hand until he thought it would fall off. "Maybelline, they did it!"

She ran into the room and hugged Tate. "I'm so happy for you two." Maybelline wiped the tears from her eyes. "We've been praying for you both. We couldn't be more thrilled."

Chester's eyes shimmered with tears. "Now, go tell our precious daughter that you both have our every blessing."

Tate figured he wore a goofy smile. "Thank you both so much. I promise to take good care of Brooke."

His smile gone, Chester whispered in Tate's ear. "Make sure you treat Brooke well, or we will have a *very* serious discussion."

Tate nodded and kept nodding. "Yes, sir. Thank you, sir." He almost saluted. "With God's help, I'll be the best husband I can to your daughter."

Chester grinned. "I'm sure you will."

Epilogue

The gentle sound of ocean waves serenaded Brooke as she breathed the salty air. Was it only yesterday she walked the aisle and pledged her love? With her past, she never thought she would have the opportunity for a new life or be given a wonderful man as a husband. Thankfully, God had other plans. She'd gone from living in the Grrrs of guilt, remorse, regret, replaying the negative, and shame to experiencing God's amazing grace.

With her back comfy against a beach chair, she yawned and opened her eyes. Brooke turned on her side and gazed at her handsome husband. "You sure did look great in your tux."

"You were gorgeous in your wedding dress." Tate grinned as he rolled over on his chair and faced her. "Then again, you are always beautiful."

Even in the sun's warmth, Brooke felt her cheeks flush with heat. "Thank you, Mr. Tillman, for marrying me."

"Are you kidding? Thank *you* for marrying me." Tate wiggled his eyebrows. "And thank you for last night."

Brooke fanned her face. "I am really enjoying marital bliss."

Tate chuckled. "I think we have a *great* start to our life together."

"I do, too." Brooke sighed. "I still can't believe how many people showed up for the wedding."

"I thought I'd never get you away from the reception since they all wanted to hug you," Tate muttered, then grinned. "I think the whole town came, and it was fun to meet your brothers and sisters and their families."

Brooke got teary-eyed just thinking about how sweet her adopted family was to her. Maybelline and Chester's natural children and grandchildren had welcomed Brooke with open arms. She didn't deserve their love or Tate's love, and she sure didn't deserve God's grace. Brooke chuckled to herself. Wasn't that what God's grace was? The unmerited favor of God. She definitely found that was true.

Tate rose out of his chair, pulled her to her feet, and kissed her. "Last one to the ocean is a rotten egg."

Brooke squealed and laughed as she ran to catch her handsome husband.

Grabbing his hand, they dove into the ocean together.

The End
of
Running from Shame

and a new beginning for Tate and Brooke.

Note from the Author

Thank you for reading *Running from Shame.* Perhaps, like Brooke, you've been trapped in the lies of the enemy and the Grrrs of guilt, remorse, regret, replaying the negative, and shame.

Whatever you've been through, whatever you've done, please go to God to receive His amazing grace and a new life in Christ. God gives new opportunities and new mercies every single day. He is a God of unfailing love who restores and repurposes messed-up lives with His redeeming grace.

"For God so [greatly] loved and dearly prized the world, that He [even] gave His [One and] only begotten Son, so that whoever believes and trusts in Him [as Savior] shall not perish, but have eternal life. For God did not send the Son into the world to judge and condemn the world [that is, to initiate the final judgment of the world], but that the world might be saved through Him." (John 3:16-17, AMP)

"If anyone is in Christ [that is, grafted in, joined to Him by faith in Him as Savior], he is a new creature [reborn and renewed by the Holy Spirit]; the old things [the previous moral and spiritual condition] have passed away. Behold,

new things have come [because spiritual awakening brings a new life]." (2 Corinthians 5:17, AMP)

"I have wiped out your wrongdoings like a thick cloud and your sins like a heavy mist. Return to Me, for I have redeemed you." "As far as the east is from the west, so far has He removed our wrongdoings from us." (Isaiah 44:22, Psalm 103:12, NASB)

"Forget the former things; do not dwell on the past. See, I am doing a new thing! Now it springs up; do you not perceive it? I am making a way in the wilderness and streams in the wasteland." (Isaiah 43:18-19, NIV)

"Forgetting those things which are behind and reaching forward to those things which are ahead, I press toward the goal for the prize of the upward call of God in Christ Jesus." (Philippians 3:13-14, NKJV)

"Let the past sleep, but let it sleep on the bosom of Christ and go out into the irresistible future with Him." ~ Oswald Chambers

Acknowledgments

First and foremost, my eternal thanks to our eternal, loving, forgiving, restoring, redeeming, wonderful God.

My sweet husband, Dennis, thank you for loving and marrying me. Thank You for your help, support, and encouragement. I'm so grateful that God blessed me with you. Je t'aime.

Patricia (Pacjac) Carroll, thank you for the critiques, feedback, and assistance. Thank you for adding fun to the writing process.

JoAnn Durgin, thank you for creating the beautiful cover. You are a blessing.

Jack Foster, thank you again for your creative Crawdad drawings used throughout the Crawdad Beach Series. (Readers, please visit Jack at jackfosterart.com).

Readers, I am very grateful to each of you. Thank you for taking the time to read *Running from Shame*.

If you liked the novel, would you be so kind as to leave a positive review and tell your friends? Thank you!

About the Author

Lisa Buffaloe is a happily married mom, speaker, and multi-published author. Lisa enjoys spending time with God, Bible study, writing, hanging out with her sweet husband, and enjoying God's beautiful nature.

Please visit Lisa at https://lisabuffaloe.com, Facebook, X(Twitter), Instagram (buffaloelisa), Amazon, or GoodReads.

Books by Lisa

Fiction

Crawdad Beach Series
Visible, yet Hidden
Running to Grace
Crystal's Journey Home
A Baker's Heart
Stella's Heart Code
River Steps Free
Mia Lets Go
A New Paige
Running from Shame

The Masterpiece Beneath
Grace for the Char-Baked

Hope and Grace Series
Nadia's Hope
Prodigal Nights
Writing Her Heart
The Discovery Chapter
Open Lens

The Fortune

Non-Fiction

Float by Faith
Heart and Soul Medication
Time with The Timeless One
The Forgotten Resting Place
Present in His Presence
We Were Meant for Paradise
One Lit Step: Devotions for your journey
The Unnamed Devotional
Flying on His Wings
Unfailing Treasures
No Wound Too Deep For The Deep Love of Christ
Living Joyfully Free Devotional (Volumes 1 & 2)

Bibliography

Oswald Chambers, *My Utmost for His Highest*, Discovery House books, Barbour Publishing, Uhrichsville, OH 44683

Running from Shame

Lisa Buffaloe

www.ingramcontent.com/pod-product-compliance
Lightning Source LLC
Chambersburg PA
CBHW051247170626
46809CB00004B/1530